I0591520

The Book of Christmas Wishes

A CLASSIC
COLLECTION
of Gamblin
CARTOONS
"4XMAS o menos

The Book of Christmas Wishes

RUNNING MAN PRESS
MICHIGAN, USA

The Book of Christmas Wishes
is published by Running Man Press

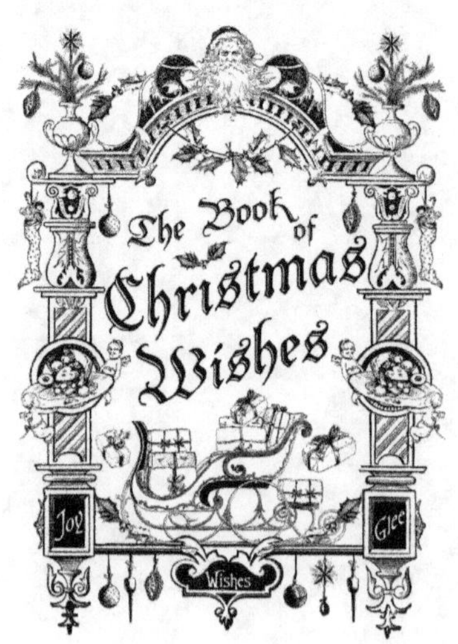

Front Cover:

Frontispiece: Bob Camblin's "A Classic Collection" Sketch

Distributed by Ingram Content Group
United States: ingramsparksupport@ingramcontent.com
Australia: ingramsparkaustralia@ingramcontent.com
International: ingramsparkinternational@ingramcontent.com

All artwork by Bob Camblin

ISBN-13: 979-8-9920123-2-3

Sketches: Bob Camblin
Ekphrastic Writing: Louis Casey

Published by Running Man Press
Royal Oak, MI U.S.A.
hello@runningmanpress.com

Other Titles by Running Man Press

Zen and the Art of Enlightenment VOL I

Zen and the Art of Enlightenment VOL II

Welcome to Santa's Read & Watch Coloring Book

Prologue by Louis Casey

Welcome, dear friend, to a realm where gingerbread men sometimes sprout legs too fragile for the North Pole workshop, where reindeer can be as mischievous as they are majestic, and where Santa himself might sail a boat along moonlit coasts—because reindeer aren't his only mode of travel! These stories may seem fanciful, but within them lies a warmth that welcomes both the youngest of dreamers and the grown-ups who still carry sparkles of childhood within their hearts.

In the pages ahead, you'll join Santa and his elves on a remarkable journey through the excitement and calm of holiday enchantment. Mortimer the Mouse, a resident artist, scampers across each chapter with a brush in his tiny paw, leaving creative footprints (or paw-prints!) in the margins. He once tried to paint Rudolph's portrait—only to discover, amid giggles, that his painting made the famous reindeer look like a trophy mount! In another story, you'll find out how a life-sized running gingerbread Santa, designed by the elves, failed spectacularly when it turned into a late-night snack for the reindeer (with Mortimer lending a few secret nibbles of his own).

Yet it's not all fun and flour. Some evenings, Santa slips quietly into an off-season reverie, wearing bright hibiscus shorts and a laid-back straw hat. The hustle of Christmas may still be months away, but his thoughts ripple with anticipation—his magical sense of who needs a little extra kindness never truly rests. Peek into those moments of reflection, and you'll see that it's not just about delivering gifts; it's about sustaining hope and wonder in a world that grows busier each day.

Though children will delight in coloring the black-and-white illustrations—spilling crayons and markers across gingerbread men, reindeer antlers, and cozy Arctic cottages—adults, too, will find their share of quiet humor and gentle wisdom folded among the pages. You might chuckle at Santa's comedic asides or find yourself relating to an elf's offbeat solution to a toy shortage. Perhaps you'll even spy a nod to the chaotic thrill of parallel universes (no one ever said Santa's magic was bound by only one reality).

Wherever you start—whether it's with Santa's dash across snowy rooftops, his seafaring sleigh coasting past oceanfront cabins, or the day he nearly lost his "Ho-Ho-Ho"—know that each tale was crafted to rekindle that soothing glow of Christmastime wonder. And if you long for a deeper look behind the scenes, each chapter offers a link to short videos brimming with extra holiday cheer.

Watch elves tinkering with prototypes or reindeer gleefully prancing under northern lights, letting you see the North Pole come to life in motion.

So gather the little ones, or settle in on your own, and pick up your colored pencils or crayons. Let the swirl of pencil lines and brushstrokes bring each North Pole adventure to vivid life, adding a splash of color to the playful sketches. The holiday spirit here belongs to everyone—child, parent, grandparent, friend—and these stories are for you all.

May this book be a cozy companion during the season of snow and stars... and may it kindle a flicker of holiday magic in your heart whenever you need it most. Whether you read these stories under twinkling Christmas lights or on a lazy summer day dreaming of winter's hush, let this be a moment of warmth and laughter, a testament that Santa's brand of joy really can last all year long.

You'll also find links to video snippets that enrich each chapter. Think of them as secret windows into North Pole life—a chance to see an elf forging a new toy design in motion, or to watch Santa himself chuckle over a mischief-making reindeer. These videos are purely optional, but if you choose to watch, you'll discover a deeper layer of enchantment woven into each bedtime reading.

Because this book doubles as a coloring book, we invite you to pick up your crayons or markers, let your imagination roam, and bring these black-and-white sketches to life. Whether you choose frosty blues and silvers to reflect winter nights or bright, candy-cane stripes in every corner, remember that your creativity fuels the same magic that keeps Santa's workshop running—wonder, playfulness, and a belief in something joyful and bright.

So find a soft blanket or cozy chair, cuddle up, and step into these stories with an open heart. Whether you're young or simply young at heart, there's a warm place for you here—where the candlelight glimmers, reindeer hooves prance on rooftops, and the quiet hum of holiday cheer lingers, just waiting for you to color it into being. Enjoy the journey, dear reader. May these pages become cherished memories in your own season of wonder.

~ Louis Casey

The Book of Christmas Wishes

EXT. REINDEER STABLES – NIGHT

SANTA, LOOKING PARTICULARLY WORN DOWN, STANDS NEXT TO PRANCER. SANTA GRIPS A ROPE, TRYING TO COAX THE RELUCTANT REINDEER FORWARD.

SANTA
C'mon, Prancer, let's go. It's Christmas Eve. We do this every year. You love this.

PRANCER
(PRANCER shakes his head, hooves firmly planted.)
Love it? Love it?! You know what I love? Not dislocating my shoulder in a wind tunnel while hauling your cookie-stuffed ass across the globe at Mach 3.

SANTA
Now, Prancer—

PRANCER
Oh, don't "Now, Prancer" me. I read the stats. Average sleigh weight has increased by 20% since 2015! What happened to the keto thing, Santa?

SANTA
That was a phase! Also, peppermint bark isn't technically a carb!

Santa tugs. Prancer doesn't budge.

PRANCER
You know who else has a union? Mall Santas. You don't see them busting their humps for nothing but an oat biscuit and a pat on the nose.
I'm done. Burnout's real, man.

SANTA
(muttering)
This is what happens when
the elves start a book club.

Behind them, BLITZEN and COMET are drinking hot toddies, watching the whole ordeal.

BLITZEN
What's the hold-up?

COMET
Prancer's on strike.

BLITZEN
Again? This is like the third time
this century.

Santa sighs and pinches the bridge of his nose.

SANTA
Fine. What do you want?

Prancer considers.

PRANCER
Better working conditions. Less weight. And one of those heated hoof massagers.

SANTA
Deal.

Prancer trots forward, triumphant.

PRANCER
Also, from now on, I pick the in-flight entertainment.

SANTA
No more eight-hour true crime podcasts.The last one made Donner paranoid about getting reindeer-napped.

PRANCER
Fine. We alternate. One of mine, one of yours.

Santa rolls his eyes and climbs into the sleigh. The other reindeer, grumbling, take their positions.

SANTA
Alright, let's get this over with.

PRANCER
So this next one's called *The Antler Conspiracy—*

SANTA
(Groaning)
I miss the old days.

As the sleigh lifts off, Mrs. Claus appears in the doorway, still scrolling on her phone.

MRS. CLAUS
Don't forget milk!

The sleigh disappears into the night.

"...it's not easy being a mythical person..."

TITLE: IT'S TOUGH BEING A MYTHICAL PERSON

INT. A DIMLY LIT BAR – LATE NIGHT

Santa Claus—though something about him looks... off—sits at the bar, hunched over a glass of something dark and brooding. His red suit is slightly unbuttoned, hat slouched, and instead of reindeer, HE has the antlers now. He sighs, takes a slow sip, then looks directly at the audience as he begins his monologue.

SANTA
(grumbling)

It's not easy being a mythical person.
You spend centuries—centuries—building a reputation, and for what?
A couple of holiday jingles and a Coca-Cola sponsorship?
Meanwhile, I'm out here pulling double duty—delivering joy
and suffering from chronic lower back pain.

SANTA (cont.)
You ever tried lugging around billions of presents while keeping your cholesterol down?
I have one cookie, and Mrs. Claus is all, "Maybe switch to oat milk, dear."
Oat milk?! I was raised on whole milk, whiskey, and raw determination!

He gestures dramatically to his new antlers.

SANTA (cont.)
And these? Don't even get me started.
Some Christmas magic mishap, they said.
Yeah, well, turns out magic is just a PR-friendly term
for "dysfunctional workplace hazard."
Do you know what it's like to wake up one morning
and become your own workforce?
I went to scratch my head and impaled my own pillow.
Dasher laughed for an hour.

Tired. He downs his drink.

SANTA (cont.)
And don't get me started on belief. The Easter Bunny?
Beloved. Tooth Fairy? Untouchable. Me? Oh, suddenly,
I'm "problematic" because I break into houses uninvited.
Listen, Kyle, I don't wanna be in your house either—I have a whole workshop,
I don't need to rummage through your fridge, OK?

He slams the glass down—gently, because Santa still has manners.

SANTA (cont.)
But kids don't believe like they used to. They've got iPads now.
They see me and go, "Uhh, your gift exchange model is inefficient,
ever heard of Amazon Prime?" I swear, one more six-year-old tries to explain
logistics to me, I'm sending them a beautifully wrapped tax bill for every unclaimed
toy they've abandoned since 2017.

Santa exhales deeply, rubbing his temples.

SANTA (cont.)
But you know what? Maybe that's the gig.
Maybe being a mythical person is just a fancy way of saying
you're a story people only care about when it's convenient.
I get one month of glory, then eleven months of obscurity.

He pauses, looks at his antlers, then gives a resigned shrug.

SANTA (cont.)
At least I finally match my team.

He laughs bitterly. The bartender (who may or may not be a disgruntled elf) slides him another drink. Santa nods in thanks, raises the glass.

SANTA (cont.)
Merry freakin' Christmas.

FADE TO BLACK

"and some of the CHILDREN are so good they are getting grenade launchers..."

TRUE, true... EVEN I'M HAVING TROUBLE traveling at NIGHT..

anomymous

INT. SANTA'S WORKSHOP – NIGHT

The workshop is less of a magical wonderland and more of a war room. The elves are exhausted, chain-smoking candy canes, and there's a "Days Since Last Incident" sign that reads 0. Santa sits on a crate labeled "UNMANNED AERIAL SYSTEMS", rubbing his temples. Across from him, an elf—his name is Jingles—clutches a clipboard, looking concerned but also kind of resigned to the madness.

JINGLES
So, uh... some of the kids were so good this year, we're giving them grenade launchers.

SANTA
(nodding, dragging on a candy cane like it's a Marlboro Red)

True... true... even I'm having trouble traveling at night.

A beat. They both stare off into the void.

JINGLES
(flipping through notes)

It's getting weird, boss. Used to be, you gave a kid a wooden train set, he was thrilled. Now it's, "Oh gee, Santa, I was hoping to get something from Anduril system to defend my treehouse from Chad."

SANTA
Chad?

JINGLES
Yeah. Chad's seven and already running a cartel out of the cul-de-sac. Got an army of Razor Scooter enforcers. We gave Timmy a slingshot last year. Chad's mom called it an "act of aggression." Now Timmy wants a flamethrower.

SANTA
(massaging his forehead)

Jesus Christ.

JINGLES
I know, right? We haven't even finished processing last year's drone strike requests.
SANTA sighs, staring at a "Nice/Naughty" list covered in redacted names.

SANTA
(grumbling)

This used to be simple. Ho-ho-ho, here's a toy truck. Here's a doll. Now I'm basically an international arms dealer in a red suit.

JINGLES
(shrugging)

The elves in R and D tried to scale it back. They released a "Anduril Peacekeeping Set."

SANTA
And?

JINGLES
Flopped. Kids said it was "too woke."

SANTA
Jesus Christ.

A loud BOOM echoes from outside. The room shakes. A terrified elf runs in, panting.

PANICKED ELF
Sir! The neighborhood militias intercepted the sleigh in Florida! We've lost Prancer!

SANTA
(standing up in horror)

You mean—

PANICKED ELF
He's defected, sir. Joined a private security firm in Texas. He's going by "Blitzenkrieg" now.

A tense silence. Santa takes a long, painful sip of eggnog straight from the carton.

SANTA
Alright. If we're doing this, we're doing this right. Prep the Roadrunners. Move the naughty list to DEFCON 2. And somebody get Frosty on the phone—he owes me a favor.

The elves scramble into action. Santa adjusts his hat, cracks his knuckles, and sighs.

SANTA
(to himself, shaking his head)

It was never about the toys... it was about sending a message.

CUT TO BLACK.

Faint sound of sleigh bells… then machine gun fire.

"...WE'RE NOT TRAVELING THIS YEAR..."

"EVERY WISH IS IN OUR CATALOGUE..

INT. NORTH POLE – SANTA'S OFFICE – NIGHT

A dimly lit office. Santa sits at his cluttered desk, flipping half-heartedly through a gigantic mail-order catalog labeled "EVERYTHING" in bold, corporate font. His once jolly eyes now carry the dead stare of a mall cop on his third energy drink. Stacks of catalogs pile up around him like paperwork in a DMV office.

Across from him, Jingles, the head elf, stands anxiously, holding a tablet. He hesitates before speaking, as if he's about to break some very bad news. Because he is.

JINGLES
So, uh, Santa... big change this year. We're... not traveling.

SANTA
(not looking up, flipping a catalog page)

Mmm. Yeah. Every wish is in our catalog.

A long pause. Jingles shifts uncomfortably.

JINGLES
Isn't this... like... your whole thing?

SANTA
(finally looking up, eyes dead inside)

You ever heard of Amazon Prime?

JINGLES
(nervous nod)

Uh, yeah. I mean, we all have.

SANTA
Yeah. That's the problem.

A beat. Jingles winces.

JINGLES
You mean…

SANTA
(nodding grimly)

I lost my contract.

Jingles clutches his tiny heart, devastated.

JINGLES
But... but Santa, you're the magic of Christmas! You bring joy! You deliver hope!

SANTA
Yeah, well, hope doesn't come with free two-day shipping.

Santa gestures to a small, greasy brown Amazon package on his desk.

SANTA
(sarcastically, waving it around)

This? This arrived before I even finished checking my list.

JINGLES
That's... concerning.

SANTA
You're telling me. I don't even remember ordering it.

A beat. They both eye the package, deeply unsettled.

JINGLES
(hesitant, tapping the catalog)

So, uh... how does this work now?

SANTA
I sit here and "approve" gifts. The catalog handles the rest.

JINGLES
(skeptical)

So... we don't make toys anymore?

SANTA
Nope. We partner with third-party sellers.

Jingles goes pale.

JINGLES
Like... dropshipping?

SANTA
(grimly nodding)

SANTA (cont.)
Like dropshipping.

Jingles physically recoils. Santa sighs and flips another page.

SANTA
(muttering)

Should've unionized in the '90s...

A knock at the door. A DELIVERY DRONE hums into the room, hovering eerily. It drops a package on Santa's desk and scans him with a red laser. A robotic voice speaks:

AMAZON DRONE
(cold, sterile)

SANTA CLAUS. WE NOTICED YOU HAVEN'T COMPLETED YOUR HOLIDAY DASH ORDERS. WOULD YOU LIKE TO ENROLL IN AUTOMATED DECISION-MAKING?

A long, horrified silence. Santa and Jingles just... stare.

SANTA
Jingles.

JINGLES
(whispering, terrified)

Yeah, boss?

SANTA
Get me my sleigh.

Jingles nods solemnly. He dashes out. Santa, grim with last-minute rebellion, slams the catalog shut. He rises. He pulls on his coat. His boots. He picks up his sleigh keys and eyes the delivery drone, which is still waiting... ominously.

SANTA
(growling, defiant)

Let's see Amazon deliver magic the way I do.

CUT TO BLACK.
Faint sound of sleigh bells... followed by the distant hum of corporate surveillance drones.

"This holiday season, don't let a billionaire in a spaceship replace the fat man in a sleigh."

HELP
WILL WORK
FOR GIFTS

EXT. CITY STREET – NIGHT
Snow falls gently over a row of luxury stores, their windows glowing with obscene amounts of Christmas lights. A massive electronic billboard flashes an ad for "Santa Prime™ – Gifts in One Hour or Your Money Back!"

PAN DOWN to reveal SANTA, standing just outside a Target, holding a handmade cardboard sign. His eyes are bloodshot, his beard is unkempt, and his red suit has seen better centuries.

SANTA
(deadpan, defeated)

You ever wake up one day and realize you've peaked?
Yeah. That's me. Santa Claus. Father Christmas. The big guy.
I had a good run. A thousand years of unchecked monopoly.
No competition. No oversight. No taxes. It was beautiful.
And now?

Gestures to sign.

SANTA (cont.)
Now I'm standing outside a Target,
hoping to trade labor for gifts like some kind of North Pole gig worker.
Do you know what it feels like to be outsourced by an app?
An app. I used to be magic, man! I defied the laws of time and space.
And now some billionaire in a hoodie can do my job
with a fleet of drones and an algorithm.
I tried to unionize the elves. You know what happened?
They got acquired. By Amazon. They have stock options now.
The North Pole is a fulfillment center.
Mrs. Claus left me for a guy who sells NFTs.
I don't even know what that is.

Pauses, rubs temples, sighs.

SANTA (cont.)
I should've pivoted to branding. Like the Easter Bunny.
You think that guy still hides eggs? No. He's got a podcast.
A sponsorship deal with Cadbury. But me?
I stuck to tradition. I believed in Christmas magic. Like an idiot.
I tried getting on Cameo. Nobody booked me.
You know who people book? The Grinch. Yeah.
Kids these days relate to the Grinch.
Because they're all chronically depressed.
Oh, and this?

Gestures to the sign, shakes head.

SANTA (cont.)
This isn't even my sign. Some guy gave it to me on his way into Best Buy.
Said I "looked like I needed it." And you know what? He's right.
You know what's worse than being unemployed?
Being irrelevant. No one's even stopping to take a selfie with me.

Watches a group of teens pass by, oblivious.

SANTA (cont.)

Nothing. They don't even recognize me.
Do you know how humiliating it is to be Santa Claus and have a kid say,
"Oh look, it's just some guy"?

SANTA (cont.)
(more animated)

JUST SOME GUY!
I INVENTED GIFT CULTURE!
I'M THE REASON YOUR CHILDHOOD HAD MEANING!

Beat. He pinches the bridge of his nose.

SANTA (cont.)
God. I should just shave the beard and move to Florida. Start over.
Be normal. Be an influencer for a new and better fad.

He exhales. Looks into the camera one last time, eyes hollow.

SANTA (cont.)
Or...
I could just burn it all down and watch Netflix.

LONG PAUSE. We hear a faint jingle of bells...

CUT TO BLACK.
A single line of text fades in:

"Merry Christmas. Try not to think too hard about it."

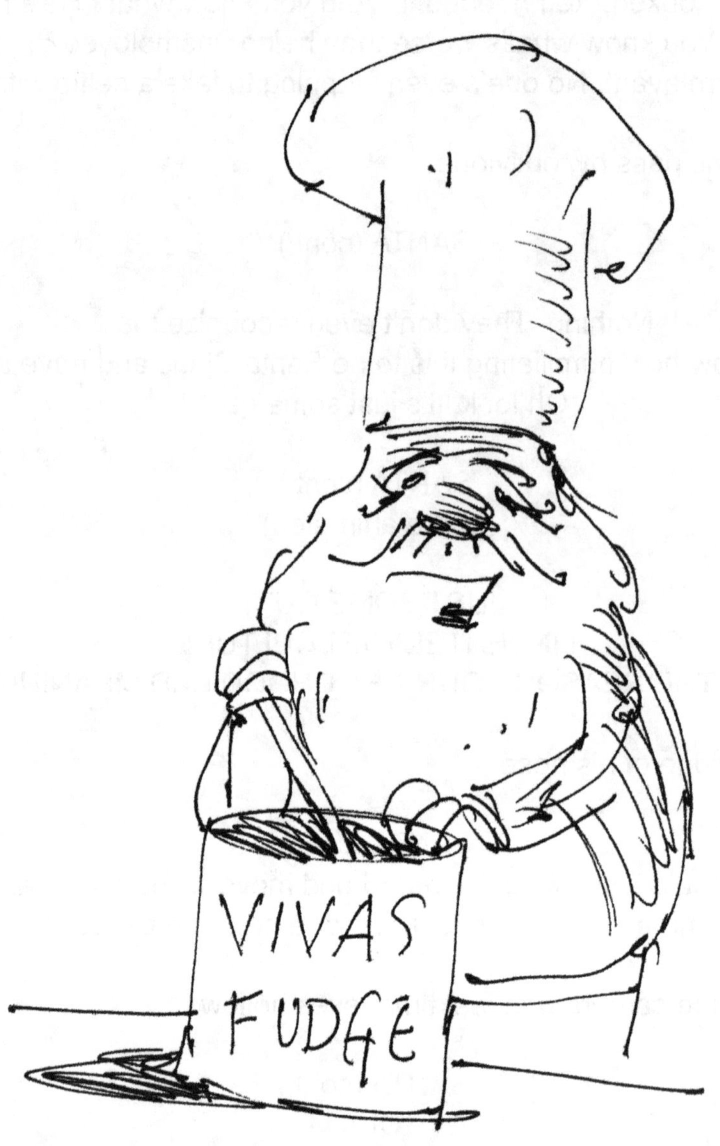
VIVAS
FUDGE

INT. SANTA'S KITCHEN – NIGHT

Soft Christmas jazz plays in the background. The kitchen is warm and cozy, lit by the soft glow of fairy lights. SANTA, wearing a chef's hat too big for his head, is hunched over a massive pot labeled "VIVA'S FUDGE," stirring slowly, like he's conjuring a spell. His brow furrows in deep concentration. This is serious business. ELVES scurry around behind him, working in the background, occasionally sneaking tastes of the fudge when Santa isn't looking.

SANTA
(softly, to himself, nostalgic)

Alright, Viva, let's see if I still remember...

He picks up a scrap of paper, handwritten in loving cursive, stained with cocoa and age.

SANTA
(reading aloud, reverent)

"One cup of sugar, one cup of love, a whole lotta butter—"

He reaches for a comically large stick of butter, dramatically tosses it into the pot. The elves gasp.

HEAD ELF
(whispers, concerned)

...that was too much butter.

SECOND ELF
(equally concerned, watching the pot)

The fudge is...changing.

The pot starts bubbling ominously. The elves take a step back.

SANTA
(ignoring them, emotional)

—"And the final touch... a spoonful of Christmas spirit."

He reaches for a jar labeled "Christmas Spirit"—which is empty. He frowns.

HEAD ELF
(nervous)

Uh, Santa? We, uh... ran out of Christmas Spirit last year.

SECOND ELF
(whispers)

Jeff Bezos bought the last batch for his boat.

SANTA stops stirring. The elves watch in fear. He stares down at the pot, looking genuinely heartbroken.

SANTA
(softly, to himself)

No Christmas Spirit… no fudge… no…

Beat. Santa closes his eyes. Then… he takes a deep breath. His face softens.

SANTA
(whispering)

Wait… I remember now.

He removes his glove, dips a single finger into the warm fudge, and tastes it.
His eyes light up. The elves lean in, tense.

SANTA
(grinning, teary-eyed)

That's it.

The elves wait for more. Santa just stands there, smiling.

HEAD ELF
(confused)

...What's it doing?

SANTA
(laughs, shaking head)

The Christmas Spirit. It's not in the jar. It's here.

He taps his chest. The elves exchange looks.

SECOND ELF
(to Head Elf, dryly)

He just means love.

HEAD ELF
(rolling eyes)

Ugh, why is everything always about love?

SANTA bursts into deep, hearty laughter. The elves groan, but they can't help but grin. They all grab spoons and dig into the fudge, laughing together as the snow falls outside.

FADE TO BLACK.

TEXT APPEARS:

"Merry Christmas. The secret ingredient is always love (...and a dangerous amount of butter)."

INT. NORTH POLE PRESS ROOM – NIGHT

A long wooden table sits at the front of the room, a microphone positioned in the center. The backdrop features an official North Pole emblem: a candy cane crossed with a peppermint. A roomful of elves, reindeer, and toy industry executives murmur, waiting for the big announcement.*

A tired, unshaven SANTA trudges to the microphone, dragging a giant poster board behind him. He slaps it onto a rickety wooden stand. The image on the board is not him. It's a perfectly airbrushed, handsome Santa. Think 1950s Coca-Cola ad Santa—crisp hat, glowing cheeks, impeccable beard.

SANTA
(clears throat, deep sigh)

Right. Listen up, folks.

The room falls silent. Santa stares at them like a man who's seen too much. He rubs his temples.

SANTA (cont.)
(gestures to the poster)

This? This guy?
This isn't me. This has never been me.

The elves nod solemnly. The reindeer exchange knowing glances.

SANTA (cont.)
(points to the poster, exasperated)

Look at this beard—perfectly fluffed.
Do you have any idea how much conditioner that takes?

HEAD ELF
(muttering)

At least two bottles…

SANTA
(ignoring him)

And the rosy cheeks? That's airbrushed.
The twinkle in the eyes? Photoshop. This man does not exist.

SANTA (cont,)
(waves hand over his own very real, exhausted body)

This…is the real Santa.

A beat. The audience takes him in. His coat is half-buttoned. His beard is slightly lopsided. His hat? Missing. His eyes? Dead inside. He leans on the podium for support like a mall Santa working overtime.

SANTA (cont.)
(suddenly emotional)

I haven't slept in a month. You know why?
Because Timmy in Oklahoma wants a PlayStation 5
and his mother wants me to teach him about the "true spirit of Christmas"—
I can't do both, Brenda.

The elves nod sympathetically. They've read Brenda's emails.

SANTA (cont.)
(getting worked up, pacing)

Every year it's the same thing: "Santa, why do you look so tired?"
"Santa, why do you smell like eggnog and regret?"
I'll tell you why. Because I AM tired.
Because I have to break into eight billion houses a night.
Because my only nutrition source is cookies and a legally questionable amount of milk.

HEAD ELF
(whispers, guilty)

We should really get him some protein…

SECOND ELF
(shrugs)

He won't eat the celery.

SANTA
(deep breath, collects himself)

Listen. I'm not saying Christmas is canceled.
I'm just saying—maybe next year, we lower the expectations.
Maybe we bring back fruit baskets.
Maybe we accept that Santa… is just a guy.

He turns back to the poster, rips it down dramatically, revealing another poster behind it—of himself, disheveled, holding a cup of really, really strong coffee, staring into the void.

SANTA (cont.)
(nods)

This? This is the new Santa!

A long silence. The crowd blinks. Then… the elves start clapping. The reindeer stomp their hooves. A single elf yells "VIVA LA SANTA!" and suddenly, the room erupts into cheers.

SANTA (cont.)
(grins, cracking his knuckles)

Alright. Now someone get me a hot chocolate. I'm taking a nap.

SANTA (cont.)
Santa is doing his best. Lower your expectations. Merry Christmas.

"...i seem to be forgetting something this year..."

INT. NORTH POLE - SANTA'S BEDROOM – NIGHT

The room is a disaster. Wrapping paper everywhere. A half-eaten gingerbread house sits on the nightstand next to a tower of coffee cups. Santa's alarm clock reads DECEMBER 24 – 11:59 PM. A frazzled, sleep-deprived SANTA stumbles around the room, rubbing his eyes. He is fully dressed from the waist up. Big red coat? Check. Big black belt? Check. No pants? Also check.

SANTA
(muttering to himself, looking around)
Alright… sack? Check.
Boots? Check.
Hat? Check.
Magic reindeer dust? Doubled up.
I'm not making that chimney mistake again.

Santa glances at himself in the mirror. His eyes squint. Something is…off. But what? He turns left. Turns right. Adjusts his beard. Nods in satisfaction.

SANTA (cont.)
(to himself, proudly)

Still got it.

He struts toward the door.

MRS. CLAUS (O.S.)
(shouting from another room)

DEAR?

SANTA
(startled, spinning around)

Wha—what?!

MRS. CLAUS appears in the doorway. Her arms are crossed. She does not look amused.

MRS. CLAUS
You forgetting something?

SANTA
(offended, scoffs)

Me? Forget something? Woman,
I've been running logistics on this operation for CENTURIES.
I know exactly what I'm doing.

MRS. CLAUS silently points down. Santa follows her finger.

A beat. A horrifying realization.

SANTA (whispers in terror)
The pants.

MRS. CLAUS stares at him. He stares back.

MRS. CLAUS (deadpan)

Are you sleep-deprived or just old?

SANTA immediately defends himself.

SANTA
(pointing aggressively)

HEY. I may be old, but I'm not… okay, I am sleep-deprived.
But still. This—this is an isolated incident.

MRS. CLAUS
(raises an eyebrow)

Uh-huh. Like last year when you put Prancer in the sleigh harness backwards?

SANTA folds his arms.

SANTA (grumbling)
It was dark.

MRS. CLAUS
Or the year before when you accidentally gave a six-year-old a chainsaw?

SANTA
(pointing a finger)
That was a clerical error.

MRS. CLAUS slowly shakes her head.

MRS. CLAUS
(softly)

…Or the time you flew to the wrong hemisphere and left gifts for the wrong children?

SANTA throws up his hands.

SANTA
OKAY, THAT one was on the eggnog.

MRS. CLAUS simply walks over, hands him his pants, and pats his cheek.

MRS. CLAUS
(smirking)

I love you, dummy.

SANTA sighs, takes the pants, and starts putting them on.

SANTA
(grumbling to himself)

This job used to be fun.

The alarm clock BEEPS—MIDNIGHT. Time to fly.

MRS. CLAUS leans in for a quick kiss. Santa, now fully dressed, grabs his sack and heads for the sleigh. As the door closes behind him, we hear one last urgent shout.

MRS. CLAUS
(O.S., shouting)

YOU'RE STILL WEARING YOUR SLIPPERS.

SANTA RE-OPENS THE DOOR.* Looks down. Sighs DEEPLY.*

SANTA
(exasperated, to himself)

I swear to god...

FADE TO BLACK.

TEXT APPEARS:

"Santa is doing his best. Lower your expectations. Merry Christmas."

..."ON the FIRST DAY of XMAS my true love gave to me..."

INT. NORTH POLE - SANTA'S WORKSHOP – NIGHT

Santa sits at his desk, looking deep in thought. His fingers drum against the table. His bushy eyebrows furrow. He is staring—intensely—at nothing. The elves are hard at work in the background, hammering, wrapping, and bickering about whose break was longer. Santa, however, is lost in a philosophical crisis.

SANTA
(muttering to himself, rubbing his temples)

On the first day of Christmas… my true love gave to me…

He pauses, squinting.

SANTA (cont.)
…A partridge in a pear tree.

A long beat. He tilts his head. Something isn't sitting right. He looks upward, confused. Above his head, a thought bubble appears. But instead of a partridge in a tree, it looks like…an eyeball with a partridge in the center.

SANTA
(mumbling, slowly)

…Why does it look like an eye?

He leans in closer. He strokes his beard. His brain is firing on all cylinders now.

SANTA
(whispering, paranoid)

…Is the partridge watching me?

He shudders. He tries to shake off the thought but can't.

SANTA
(muttering, defensive)

No, no. That's ridiculous. A bird can't judge me.

He glances up at the thought bubble again. The partridge… looks judgmental.

SANTA
(gasps; accusing, pointing at the sky)

You think you're better than me?!

An elf pauses, confused. He looks at Santa, then up at nothing, then back at Santa.

ELF
Uh... boss? You good?

SANTA waves him off, still staring at the partridge-in-an-eye illusion, suspicious.

SANTA
What does it mean? What is my true love trying to tell me?

ELF
(glancing at another elf, whispering)

Should we… call Mrs. Claus?

Santa is now full-on spiraling. He stands up, paces the room, waving his hands dramatically.

SANTA
(ranting)

Is the partridge in the tree—or is the tree in the partridge?
Is Christmas watching me? Am I the partridge? WHO AM I?!

The elves, now thoroughly uncomfortable, slowly start backing away. Santa grabs his beard, pacing faster.

SANTA
(whispers, dark realization)

Oh god. It's all a test.

He stops. He spins around dramatically.

SANTA
(pointing at no one in particular)

SOMEONE GET ME A DICTIONARY AND A THERAPIST.

The elves scatter. Cut to Mrs. Claus in the next room, sipping cocoa. She hears the commotion, sighs, and grabs a bottle of wine.

"Merry Christmas. Question everything. But maybe not this much."

Santa's list,
this year,
will be
SMALLER
he is oney
giving to
the one's
with a
recognized
CRETIT CARD
XMAS
Amenos
'91
anonymous

INT. NORTH POLE – SANTA'S OFFICE – NIGHT

A cluttered desk stacked with letters from children. Santa sits, scowling at a computer screen. He clicks furiously at an online form. His hat is slightly askew, his beard disheveled. His eyes dart between a stack of wish lists and a credit card verification page.

SANTA
(muttering, reading aloud)

"Ho, ho, ho! Welcome to the new streamlined North Pole Wish Fulfillment Program.
Due to global logistics disruptions, rising reindeer fuel costs,
and a recent incident involving an elf union strike,
all gifts now require pre-approved financial backing.

Santa rubs his temples. He takes a deep breath and clicks a button. The screen spins. Then—BEEP!

SANTA
(reading, horrified)

"Card declined."

Santa leans back, stunned. He slowly turns to an elf assistant, who looks nervous as hell.

SANTA
(pointing at screen, voice rising)

DO YOU MEAN TO TELL ME… that Timmy Jenkins, age six,
who asked for a bike, some LEGOs, and—and I'm quoting here—"peace on Earth"…
was JUST DENIED BECAUSE HIS MOM'S CREDIT CARD EXPIRED?!

NERVOUS ELF
(cautiously chewing on a candy cane)

Uh… Yeah, boss. We, uh… We switched to pay-to-play this year.
Y'know, like Disney Plus.

SANTA
(deadpan, blinking slowly)

…You're telling me Christmas has a subscription plan now?

NERVOUS ELF
(shrugging, nodding)

Yeah. Santa Prime.

SANTA collapses into his chair. He stares at the ceiling, then glances at his old, worn parchment list of "Nice" and "Naughty" children. He holds it reverently. Then, slowly, he tears it in half.

SANTA
(muttering, shaking head)

I knew the spirit of Christmas would die,
but I thought I'd at least outlive RadioShack.

He gestures to the screen, the endless database of credit-scored wish lists. The elf winces. Santa leans forward. His face darkens.

SANTA
(growling)

THIS IS WHAT IT'S COME TO, HUH?!
NOT NAUGHTY OR NICE—JUST CREDITWORTHY OR DENIED?!

NERVOUS ELF
(small voice)

Uh... yeah. Also, um... we're doing surge pricing on Christmas Eve.

SANTA FREEZES. His eye twitches.

SANTA
(whispers, broken)

...Surge pricing?

NERVOUS ELF
(nods, now terrified)

Yeah. Last-minute wish fulfillment fees. It's... y'know... market-driven.

SANTA grabs a snow globe off his desk and YEETS it across the room. The elf ducks. The snow globe smashes against the wall, sending tiny figurines of Santa and his sleigh flying.

SANTA
(fuming, pacing)

I'M MARKET-DRIVEN! I'VE BEEN DRIVING THE MARKET FOR CENTURIES!

Santa grabs a candy cane from his desk, bites off the end aggressively. He gestures wildly. The elf backs up.

SANTA
(ranting, full meltdown)

IT USED TO BE SIMPLE! "MAKE A LIST, CHECK IT TWICE."
NOW I GOTTA RUN A FICO SCORE ON A TODDLER
JUST TO DROP OFF A DAMN TEDDY BEAR!

NERVOUS ELF
(weak smile)

Yeah, well, banks do it.

SANTA pauses. He slowly turns. His eye twitches harder. The elf realizes he should not have said that.

SANTA
(dead serious, voice low)

...Did you just compare me... to a bank?

NERVOUS ELF
(sweating, backing up)

Uh... um... No?

SANTA cracks his knuckles. The elf RUNS OUT OF THE ROOM. Santa throws his hat on the desk. He sighs, defeated. Then, after a long pause—

SANTA
(grumbling, typing into computer)

Guess I'll apply for a bailout.

FADE TO BLACK.

SANTA (cont.)

Merry Christmas. Your wish is pending third-party financing.

GOOD

BAD

INT. NORTH POLE – SANTA'S OFFICE – NIGHT

A dimly lit office. Santa sits at his desk, hands folded, sweating. Before him, a long parchment list. Above it, a pendulum swings in chaotic loops. It hovers over two boxes: "GOOD" and "BAD." Santa's eyes dart nervously as the pendulum oscillates wildly.

SANTA
(muttering to himself, watching pendulum)

Alright… Alright… Deep breath, big guy.
You've been doing this for centuries. No pressure.
Just deciding the moral worth of every child on Earth based on zero context.
Easy.

The pendulum spins violently, forming an infinity loop between GOOD and BAD. Santa grimaces.

SANTA (cont.)
(gritting teeth)

"Oh, for the love of—WOULD YOU JUST PICK A SIDE?!"

The pendulum slows slightly, hovering over "GOOD." Santa sighs in relief—until it snaps back to BAD. His eye twitches.

SANTA (cont.)
(groaning, rubbing temples)

I don't even know why I bother anymore! Morality isn't binary! What if Timmy stole a candy bar but also helps his grandma with groceries? WHAT THEN, PENDULUM?

The pendulum just keeps spinning. Santa slams his fist on the desk. An elf assistant pokes his head in.

NERVOUS ELF
(chewing on a candy cane)

Uh… hey, boss? Quick update on Timmy Jenkins.

SANTA
(without looking up, defeated)

Did he steal another candy bar?

NERVOUS ELF
(nodding)

Yeah… but he also rescued a kitten. So, y'know, classic moral paradox.

SANTA glares at the pendulum, then at the elf. He gestures wildly at the list.

SANTA
(mocking, frustrated)

"Oh, sure, let's let some MAGICAL OFFICE SUPPLY
decide if Timmy gets a PS5 or a lump of existential coal!

NERVOUS ELF
(hesitantly)

...We could... I dunno... go case by case?

SANTA FREEZES. The room goes dead silent. He slowly turns. His beard bristles. His hands tremble. The elf immediately realizes his mistake.

SANTA
(low, dangerous voice)

...Case by case.

NERVOUS ELF
(backpedaling hard)

I—I mean—totally a dumb idea! Haha! Just kidding!

SANTA
(voice rising)

YOU WANT ME TO INDIVIDUALLY EVALUATE SEVEN BILLION PEOPLE?!
ARE YOU INSANE?! DO I LOOK LIKE A SUPREME COURT JUSTICE?!

NERVOUS ELF
(sweating, panicking)

NOPE.
No. No, sir. You look like a... a... very, uh... jolly man... who is... fully in control of his life.
SANTA slams both hands on the desk. He laughs bitterly.
He gestures to the pendulum, still spinning.
He points wildly at his own face.

SANTA
(screaming, manic laughter)

OH, DO I?! DO I LOOK JOLLY?! BECAUSE I'VE HAD THREE HOURS OF SLEEP, AND I'M ARGUING WITH A GHOST PENDULUM ABOUT WHETHER SHOPLIFTING CANCELS OUT GOOD GRADES!

SANTA grabs his Santa hat, yanks it off, and THROWS it across the room. He breathes heavily. The elf stares, terrified.

SANTA (cont.)
(muttering to himself, pacing)

I need a drink. I need several drinks. Maybe a whole bottle of—

NERVOUS ELF
(quickly)

Oh! Uh…! No drinking this year, sir. Mrs. Claus put you on holiday detox.

SANTA FREEZES. His face darkens. The pendulum stops. He stares straight ahead.

SANTA
(whispering, broken)

…What.

NERVOUS ELF
(shrinking)

Y-yeah, um… She said "for your health" or something? No eggnog, no bourbon, no "reindeer fuel," no cinnamon whiskey.

SANTA SLOWLY SITS. He rests his face in his hands. The pendulum begins spinning again. The elf nervously backs out.

NERVOUS ELF (cont.)
(calling from the hallway)

Anyway, uh… we'll just mark Timmy as "Pending Review."

SANTA looks up. He laughs hysterically. The pendulum spins into a blur.

SANTA
(manic, shouting at ceiling)

PENDING REVIEW?! THAT'S NOT A MORAL CATEGORY!
THAT'S A BANK LOAN STATUS!

FADE TO BLACK.

SANTA (cont.)
If morality is this confusing, maybe we all deserve coal.

WANTED

INT. SHERIFF'S OFFICE – WANTED POSTER WALL – NIGHT

A dimly lit sheriff's office in some forgotten desert town. The camera pans across wanted posters: OUTLAWS. BANK ROBBERS. HORSE THIEVES. Then—SANTA CLAUS. The poster reads: "WANTED." Santa's haggard, wrinkled, and haunted. A grizzled SHERIFF squints at it.

SHERIFF
(chewing on a toothpick, reading aloud)

...Wanted for multiple counts of breaking and entering... Grand theft pastry... Illegal reindeer racing... And—"Flying under the influence?!

A nervous DEPUTY (mid-20s, over-eager, wildly out of his depth) flips through a thick case file.

DEPUTY
(reading from file)

Sir, I—I think we've got enough to put him away for life.
Look at this rap sheet! Trespassing in every country.
Fraudulent identity—his real name's Saint Nicholas, but he goes by Kris Kringle,
Father Christmas, and Sinterklaas in Belgium! Multiple aliases!
That's mafia behavior!

SHERIFF
(grunting, nodding)

Yeah, real sketchy. Also, why does this guy never age?
I mean, look at him!
Either we're dealin' with a supernatural entity
or a Russian botched cloning experiment.

DEPUTY
(leaning in, lowering voice)

Or... he made a deal with the devil.

SHERIFF
(scoffing)

Oh please. If Santa sold his soul,
he'd at least get a better distribution system.
Look at Amazon! One-day delivery.
Santa? One night, once a year. Guy's an amateur.

The deputy shuffles through more papers. He gasps.

DEPUTY
(pointing at file, whispering)

Sir… this just came in from Interpol.

SHERIFF
(reading, eyes widening)

…Oh. Oh, sweet baby Jesus.

The camera zooms in on the file. The charges pile up:

Animal Cruelty – Whipping Reindeer Across the Globe.
Illegal Chimney Access.
Data Privacy Violations – Keeping Lists of Who's Naughty or Nice.
Exploitation of Non-Unionized Elf Labor.

SHERIFF
(leaning back, rubbing temples)

Okay, that last one? That one's bad. I mean, elf labor violations?
We're talking sweatshop-level conditions.
Zero wages. No healthcare. No pensions.

DEPUTY
(reading further, gasping again)

Sir. Sir. There's more. He's been caught on multiple traffic cameras
doing Mach 3 speeds over major cities.
FAA's after him. Homeland Security says they can't track him.

SHERIFF
(stunned)

This… this is worse than I thought.

DEPUTY
(panicking)

Do we send out an APB? Do we call in NATO?

SHERIFF
(thinking, serious tone)

No. We do nothing.

DEPUTY
(shocked)

What?!

SHERIFF
(dead serious, lowering voice)

Son, let me ask you something. Who do you think really runs the world?

The deputy blinks. The sheriff leans forward, voice a whisper.

SHERIFF
(darkly)

The Coca-Cola Company.

Silence. The deputy shivers. He slowly looks at Santa's WANTED POSTER. His eyes widen. The red suit. The white beard. The smiling, corporate-approved face.

DEPUTY
Oh my god.

SHERIFF
Yeah. Oh my god.

DEPUTY
(frantic, sweating)

If we go after Santa, we go after Christmas.
If we go after Christmas, we go after Big Soda. If we go after Big Soda, we—

SHERIFF
(nodding, finishing the thought)

—disappear.

They sit in absolute silence. The deputy looks around nervously. The sheriff stares at the WANTED poster. Then, slowly, he tears it down. He lights a match. The flames devour it.

SHERIFF
(whispering, staring into the fire)

Nobody… arrests Santa.

"Coca-Cola: Bringing You Christmas Since 1931."

¿"genuine sightings!"

—sunsay

INT. BASEMENT – CONSPIRACY THEORIST'S LAIR – NIGHT

A dimly lit basement filled with newspaper clippings, red strings connecting dots on a corkboard, and an overworked espresso machine wheezing in the corner. At the center, a haggard conspiracy theorist—think Charlie Day from "Always Sunny" meets Lewis Black on a bad day—paces frantically in front of a projection screen. On it? The image of "Genuine Sightings" Santa.

CONSPIRACY THEORIST
(wild-eyed, frenzied, pointing at Santa's face on the screen)

Alright, listen up, sheeple! You've been lied to.
Lied to since birth! They said he's a myth,
a children's story, a seasonal marketing gimmick.
But I have proof.

He slaps a grainy black-and-white Polaroid onto the corkboard.

CONSPIRACY THEORIST
(screaming)

Genuine Sightings!

A nervous intern, assigned here against his will, shifts uncomfortably in his chair.

INTERN
(cautious)

Uh... okay?

CONSPIRACY THEORIST
(mocking him)

"Uh, okay?" That's your reaction? Buddy, open your mind! I've been tracking Santa Claus for twenty years. Twenty. Years.

INTERN
(mumbling, reading notes)

It says here you've also been banned from three malls...

CONSPIRACY THEORIST
(ignoring him, continuing his rant)

You ever wonder why NORAD tracks Santa every year?
Huh? You ever stop and question that?! A government-funded military radar system...
tracking a man who supposedly "doesn't exist?"

INTERN
(nervous, shifting in chair)

I think that's just… a fun thing for kids?

CONSPIRACY THEORIST
(laughing maniacally, pacing)

Oh, oh sure! "A fun thing for kids!"
Like fluoride in the water! Or daylight savings time!
Open your sheeple eyes!

He pulls out a yellowed newspaper clipping and slaps it onto the corkboard.

CONSPIRACY THEORIST
(pointing at headline)

1932 – MASS SIGHTINGS IN NEW YORK CITY.
Witnesses claim a rotund man in red broke into their homes,
left behind gifts, ate cookies, and vanished. That's a felony. Multiple felonies.

INTERN
(hesitant)

I mean, yeah, if that actually happened, sure…

CONSPIRACY THEORIST
(interrupting, dramatic pause)

But they never arrested him.

INTERN
(blinking)

Because… he doesn't exist?

CONSPIRACY THEORIST
(slamming hands on desk)

OR BECAUSE HE'S ABOVE THE LAW?!

He throws down a blurry, out-of-focus photo of Santa Claus walking through a parking lot holding a Starbucks cup.

CONSPIRACY THEORIST
(whispering, dramatic)

2019. Ohio. A man in a red suit. White beard.
He was seen buying a pumpkin spice latte.

INTERN
(leaning in, confused)

...So?

CONSPIRACY THEORIST
(pointing aggressively at the photo)

SANTA. DOESN'T. NEED. COFFEE.

INTERN
(staring, processing this insanity)

...You think Santa's real because you saw a bearded man at Starbucks?

CONSPIRACY THEORIST
(throwing a pile of photos at the intern's face)

That's just the tip of the iceberg!
You think it's a coincidence that Santa wears red and white?
He gestures wildly. Coca-Cola. You think it's a coincidence
that he works one night a year?
He slaps another photo onto the board. Jeff Bezos.

INTERN
(staring at the board, blinking)

Wait... you're saying Santa is in league with Jeff Bezos?

CONSPIRACY THEORIST
(nodding, whispering)

That's how they get the one-day delivery.
A tense beat. The intern leans back in his chair. He's officially in too deep. The conspiracy theorist leans in closer.

CONSPIRACY THEORIST
(low voice)

You wanna know what sealed the deal for me? The final piece of the puzzle?

INTERN
(numb, defeated)

Sure.

The conspiracy theorist slowly holds up a blurry security cam image of a chimney. The timestamp reads December 25, 2022, 2:14 AM. A giant boot is visible descending down the chimney.

CONSPIRACY THEORIST
(dead serious)

That's not a bird. That's not a plane. That's not even Elon Musk's dumbass rocket.

INTERN
(staring at the photo, exhausted)

...That's probably a raccoon.

A long, painful silence. The conspiracy theorist narrows his eyes. The intern rubs his temples.

CONSPIRACY THEORIST
(hissing)

You're on the naughty list.

FADE TO BLACK.

CONSPIRACY THEORIST
Santa does exist. But he's not a jolly old man.
He's a corporate-backed, coffee-drinking, Bezos-funded enigma.
And he knows where you live.

i am not ARMED...

INT. AIRPORT SECURITY CHECKPOINT – NIGHT

A tired, frazzled Santa Claus shuffles through the security line, dragging an overstuffed red sack behind him. He yawns, removes his boots, and places them in a plastic bin. A TSA AGENT, a humorless man in his 50s, eyes him skeptically.

TSA AGENT
Sir, I'm gonna need you to remove your coat and step through the scanner.

SANTA
(annoyed, muttering)

Ho-ho-holy hell, this again…

Santa removes his massive coat, revealing an equally massive belly. He shuffles through the scanner. The alarm BLARES.

TSA AGENT
Sir, step back. Any metal on you?

SANTA
(gesturing to himself)

Yeah. A giant belt buckle, a lifetime of regret,
and about forty pounds of cookies.

TSA AGENT
Step aside. Arms out.

Santa reluctantly lifts his arms as another TSA agent pats him down. They stop abruptly at his stomach.

TSA AGENT
What's in here?

SANTA
Uh… Christmas spirit?

TSA AGENT
(deadpan)

Gonna need you to be more specific.

A SUPERVISOR approaches, looking at Santa's ID.

SUPERVISOR
Sir, this ID says your name is… Kris Kringle?

Also goes by Saint Nicholas, Father Christmas, and Sinterklaas?

SANTA
I get around.

TSA AGENT
So you're telling me you deliver gifts to millions of homes overnight?
With no known point of origin?

SANTA
Exactly.

TSA AGENT
...Sounds like smuggling to me.

SANTA
Smuggling?! Buddy, I don't even charge for this stuff! Have you seen
how much I give away for free? I am literally the worst businessman in history.

SUPERVISOR
Sir, you were last seen breaking and entering into multiple homes worldwide.

SANTA
Oh, COME ON. Those people want me in their homes.
You think kids leave out cookies for a burglar?

TSA AGENT
And what's in that sack?

SANTA
Toys, mostly.

TSA AGENT
Toys?

SANTA
What, you think I'm running guns?

TSA Agent exchanges a glance with the supervisor. Santa open his sack dramatically.

SANTA
Look! A stuffed bear, a Nintendo Switch, a PS5—
if I could actually smuggle those, I'd be a billionaire.

SUPERVISOR
Sir, I'm going to need you to step aside for a full-body scan.

SANTA
(grumbling, stepping into the scanner)

Unbelievable. This is the thanks I get? The guy who delivers joy to children?
The guy who gives Jeff Bezos competition for one day a year?!

TSA agent glances at the screen, raises an eyebrow.

TSA AGENT
Sir, are you aware you have eight unidentified objects trailing you?

SANTA
Oh. Yeah. Those are my reindeer.

TSA AGENT
Sir, we do not allow livestock past security.

SANTA
(annoyed)

Buddy, they fly.

SUPERVISOR
(deep sigh)

Sir, we're gonna need to take you to secondary screening.

SANTA
Fine! But if you guys put me on the No Fly List,
literally every child in the world is gonna riot.

TSA AGENT
Oh, don't worry. You can still fly commercial.

SANTA
Oh, great. So I get to spend Christmas Eve in economy
next to a guy eating a tuna sandwich?

SUPERVISOR
Sir, you have the right to remain silent.

SANTA
Yeah? Well, so do all the naughty kids.

SANTA (cont.)
And that's why I started using Santa Prime!

1993
OFF
ON
seasonsgreetings

It was the night before Christmas, and the North Pole was quiet—eerily quiet. The elves had finished wrapping, the reindeer were in their stables, and the last letter had been read.

Santa sat alone at his wooden desk, staring at the great holiday switch before him. A simple lever, labeled OFF and ON. It controlled all of it—the warmth, the wonder, the joy.

Every year, he flipped this switch, and the world woke up to Christmas morning. Stockings filled, trees glowed, cookies mysteriously vanished. It was all part of the magic. But tonight... Santa hesitated.

He rubbed his beard, deep in thought. What if—just for once—Christmas didn't come?

Would the world notice? Would people still laugh and hug and sing, or had Christmas become just another flick of a switch?

He sighed, glancing at the glowing NOEL sign above. Maybe Christmas wasn't about the switch. Maybe it was about the kids holding their breath before tearing through wrapping paper, the parents whispering "go back to bed" at 5 a.m., the feeling of belonging when the snow fell just right.

His hand tightened on the lever.

With a deep breath, he smiled. Click.

And just like that, the world filled with Christmas.

Lights twinkled, chimneys rumbled, and laughter rang through the snowy streets. Somewhere, a child woke up too early, a dog barked at wrapping paper, and a grandparent reached for their favorite ornament with a wistful grin.

Christmas wasn't in the switch.

It had been on all along.

Gifts
GOOD
BAD

It was the night before Christmas, and deep inside the North Pole, in a warm and cozy office, Santa Claus sat at his big wooden desk. A small candle flickered beside him, casting long shadows on the stone walls. Snow swirled outside the frosted windows, and in the distance, the faint sound of elves hammering, wrapping, and giggling could be heard.

Santa let out a deep, jolly sigh as he adjusted his glasses and peered down at the most important machine in the entire workshop—the Sorting Desk.

This was no ordinary desk. No, no, no! This desk was magic. On its surface were two arrows: one pointing left to the Good Pile and one pointing right to the Bad Pile. The sign in the middle, written in Santa's finest calligraphy, simply read: GIFTS.

Now, Santa had a special rule when it came to sorting presents. Every child in the world had their name written on a tiny slip of parchment, and as each name appeared before him, he would take a deep breath and listen—listen to the whispers of kindness, laughter, and the good deeds the child had done that year.

If a child had been very good, their name would glow with golden light, and the parchment would gently float into the Good Pile on its own.

But if a child had been a little naughty—perhaps they pulled their sister's pigtails, or hid their vegetables under the rug—then Santa would rub his beard and say, "Oh dear, we all make mistakes!" And he would think about all the nice things they had done too. If their kindness outweighed their mischief, then Santa would give a nod, and the parchment would land safely in the Good Pile.

But then, there were the tricky ones. The ones who had been very, very naughty. Maybe they had thrown a tantrum over a toy, or refused to share, or—worst of all—forgotten to say "please" and "thank you" all year long. Those names would tremble slightly as if they knew what was coming.

Santa would sigh, shake his head, and with a soft flick of his fingers, those names would plop into the Bad Pile.

Now, here was the secret that only Santa and his elves knew: Even the Bad Pile got gifts!

Not regular gifts, of course. No shiny new toys, no teddy bears, no peppermint-striped candy canes. Instead, those children would receive The Coal of Reflection.

You see, this wasn't ordinary coal! It was magic coal. When a naughty child held it in their hands, it would make them feel just a little bit guilty—not too much, just enough. Enough to remind them that being kind was always the better choice. And, if they really thought about their actions and tried to be good, something magical would happen…

The coal would vanish!
And in its place, a tiny golden bell would appear, ringing softly as a promise—a promise that next year, they would do better.

As Santa continued sorting, the elves peeked into his office. "Everything all right, Santa?" asked Twinkle, the smallest of them all.

Santa chuckled and leaned back in his chair. "Everything is just as it should be," he said with a wink.

And with that, the last name was placed in its pile, and the sleigh bells rang outside. It was time for Santa to go!

He stood up, stretched his arms, and with a deep, booming Ho Ho Ho! he grabbed his sack and stepped out into the snowy night.

With one final look back at his Sorting Desk, he smiled. Because Christmas wasn't just about gifts —it was about learning, about growing, and most of all, about the magic of second chances.

And with that, he was off into the starry sky, ready to deliver joy to every child, good and naughty alike.

¿WHADAYUMEAN,' NO MOR HO-HO-HO!

The night was crisp, and the sky shimmered with stars, but something was very, very wrong at the North Pole. Santa Claus stood in the snowy clearing, dressed in his warmest red coat, his fluffy hat slightly askew. He blinked at the reindeer standing in front of him, his old, twinkling eyes wide with confusion.

SANTA
What do you mean no more ho-ho-ho?

The reindeer, a tall and noble creature with antlers like great twisted branches, stomped his hoof in the snow. His breath puffed in little clouds as he shook his head.

RUDOLPH
Santa, we need to talk.

SANTA
Not another reindeer meeting!

Every year, the elves had their meetings about fair wages in candy canes. The gingerbread men went on strike once over cookie quality control. And now, the reindeer?

RUDOLPH
(clearing his throat)

We've been pulling this sleigh for centuries, Santa.
It's exhausting! Snowstorms, rooftop landings, dodging airplanes—it's a lot!"

SANTA
(stroking his beard)

But it's Christmas Eve!

RUDOLPH
(narrowing his eyes)

Exactly. Why do you get all the Ho-Ho-Ho's and we get all the heavy lifting?
Dasher's back is sore. Dancer has ice in his hooves.
Rudolph's nose is tired of guiding this operation!"

Santa rubbed his temples. He looked around at the other reindeer standing in a picket line, tiny protest signs hanging from their antlers. Santa sighed. He knew when he was outnumbered.

SANTA
So… what do you want?

The reindeer whispered among themselves. Finally, the leader turned back to Santa.

RUDOLPH
A warm-up room with heated floors.

SANTA
(nodding)

Reasonable.

RUDOLPH
Unlimited hot cocoa with extra marshmallows.

SANTA
Done

RUDOLPH
And from now on, YOU have to say the Ho-Ho-Ho's for us!

SANTA
I already do that.

RUDOLPH
Yeah, but we want enthusiasm. We want big, hearty Ho-Ho-Ho's from the gut!

Santa took a deep breath, planted his boots in the snow, and let out the loudest, jolliest "HO! HO! HO!!!" the world had ever heard.

The snow on the rooftops shook. The Christmas lights flickered. Penguins in the South Pole stopped what they were doing and looked north.

RUDOLPH
(nodding approvingly)

Alright. Let's fly.

And just like that, the strike was over.

The sleigh was loaded, the bells jingled, and Santa climbed aboard, his cheeks still flushed from that grand Ho-Ho-Ho.

And as they soared into the starry night, Santa couldn't help but chuckle to himself.

SANTA
Maybe next year, I'll ask for a reindeer union contract in advance.

And so, Christmas was saved once again.

"...we didnt even have reindeer that year..."

"IN THE WINTER of

It was the coldest winter in the North Pole's history.

The snow fell in thick, heavy blankets, piling up so high that even the tallest candy cane poles disappeared beneath the white. The stars twinkled above the frozen land, casting silver light on Santa's workshop. But inside, there was a problem.

A BIG problem.

Santa's reindeer had all come down with a case of the Sniffling Antler Flu. Their noses ran more than Rudolph's ever glowed, and their sneezes sent tinsel flying through the air like confetti. They huddled in the stables under heavy wool blankets, sipping hot cocoa through peppermint straws. Even Dasher, the fastest of them all, could barely get up to a light jog.

"Well, that's it then," sighed one of the elves. "No Christmas this year."

Santa rubbed his chin and shook his head. "No Christmas?" he said. "Ho, ho, NO!"

"But Santa," said Jingle, the elf in charge of sleigh operations. "The sleigh is way too heavy to carry all by yourself!"

Santa laughed and patted his belly. "Nonsense! This is what I've been training for!"

Now, if you must know, Santa had been sneaking in a little exercise between cookie breaks.

He'd been lifting toy sacks like they were weights.
He'd been practicing jumps over scattered gift boxes.
And every morning, he took a lap around the workshop—okay, maybe a half lap (and maybe he stopped for a cinnamon roll halfway through).
But tonight? Tonight, Santa would RUN CHRISTMAS.

The Great Rooftop Dash

With a sack slung over his shoulder and a determined twinkle in his eye, Santa dashed off into the night.

He leaped from rooftop to rooftop, gripping chimneys for balance.
He skidded across frozen shingles, barely stopping himself from tumbling into the snow.
He hopped fences, rolled through gardens, and at one point, had to wrestle a particularly aggressive inflatable snowman out of his way.

Down the chimneys he went, faster than ever.
Plop! A toy train under the tree.
Plop! A teddy bear next to the stockings.
Whoosh! Cookies into his mouth (no time to waste!).

By the time Santa reached the last house, his boots were smoking from all the running. He plopped the final present under the tree and wiped the sweat from his brow.

And then—just as he turned to leave—he saw it.

A small note, taped to the plate of half-eaten cookies.

"Dear Santa,
Thanks for all the toys every year! But I hope YOU get a present too.
Love, Mia"

Santa smiled. That was the best present he could ever receive.

The Return to the North Pole

As the sun began to rise, Santa finally trudged back into the workshop, his suit covered in soot, his beard tangled with twigs, and his boots completely worn out.

The elves gasped. "Santa! What happened?!"

Santa chuckled as he collapsed into his chair. "We didn't even have reindeer that year!" he boomed. "But Christmas still made it!"

The elves cheered. The reindeer cheered from their beds. And Mrs. Claus? She shoved a plate of warm gingerbread cookies in Santa's hands.

"Eat first," she said, "Tell stories later."

And as Santa took his first bite, he thought to himself—

Running Christmas was fun… but next year, the reindeer were definitely getting a flu shot.

"OF COURSE I'LL FIT...
...WORKED OUT WITH
THE ELVES THIS SOMMER..."

It was Christmas Eve, and Santa Claus stood atop a snowy rooftop, hands on his belly, peering at a very, very small chimney pipe. A thin wisp of smoke curled from the top, like a little ribbon dancing in the cold night air.

"Hmm," Santa muttered, scratching his fluffy beard. "That's... a little smaller than I remember."

He adjusted his belt, took a deep breath, and then reassured himself, "Of course I'll fit. I worked out with the elves this summer!"

Now, it was true—Santa had spent the summer doing jumping jacks with Jolly Jack, the most energetic elf in the North Pole. He had also lifted presents with the strongest elf, Burly Bernard. And let's not forget about yoga lessons with Tinsel Tasha, who had him bending like a candy cane!

But... that was months ago. And there had been a lot of cookies since then.

Santa took another deep breath and patted his round belly.

"Alright, here we go!" he said.

He wiggled one boot into the chimney, then another. Then, with a great big inhale—WHOOSH!—he disappeared down the pipe.

For a moment, all was silent.

Then... CLANK. THUD. OOF!

Inside the house, a little girl named Emily had been listening for sleigh bells when she suddenly heard a muffled "Uh-oh..." from the fireplace.

She tiptoed toward the chimney and whispered, "Santa?"

A small poof of soot floated down, and Santa's voice echoed from above.

"Hello there! Don't mind me! Just a little... stuck!"

Emily giggled and ran to get a plate of cookies.

"Santa," she said, holding up a cookie to the chimney, "maybe this will help!"

There was a long pause. Then Santa's voice chuckled.

"Oh, Emily, you're very kind! But I think more cookies might be the problem here!"

Emily thought for a moment. Then she had an idea.
She ran back to the kitchen, grabbed the bottle of magic Christmas milk (the one she had set out just in case Santa needed extra strength), and poured a glass.

"Here you go, Santa! This will give you a boost!"

There was a loud GULP!, followed by a great, big POP!, and then—FWOMP!—Santa tumbled out of the fireplace in a burst of soot and sparkles.

He sat up, blinking, his red suit covered in little gray puffs.

Emily clapped her hands. "You did it!"

Santa dusted himself off and gave her a wink. "With a little Christmas magic and a very smart helper."

Then he reached into his sack, pulled out a beautifully wrapped present, and handed it to her.

"Merry Christmas, Emily."

With a twinkle in his eye, he placed a finger alongside his nose, and in the blink of an eye—POOF!—he was gone.

Emily ran to the window just in time to see Santa soaring into the night, his sleigh bells ringing as he called out:

"Merry Christmas to all, and to all a good night!"

MERRY
CHRISTMAS

The world was quiet on Christmas Eve, snowflakes falling in a slow, sleepy drift. Lights twinkled in windows, stockings hung expectantly, and children everywhere were curling up under their blankets, dreaming of the morning to come.

But far away—far beyond the snowy rooftops and chimneys—Santa Claus was not where you'd expect him to be.

He wasn't guiding his sleigh through the night sky. He wasn't double-checking the Nice and Naughty List. And he certainly wasn't squeezing himself down chimneys.

Instead, he was sitting on the grassy banks of a lake, the moon and sun hanging side by side in the sky, as if neither of them could decide who should be in charge. Santa was dressed not in his usual red coat, but in a cozy fishing vest, his hat tipped to the side, and his old boots propped up on a log. He held a long fishing pole in his hands, the line dipping lazily into the water.

He gave a contented sigh.

"Ahhhh...," he stretched his arms wide, his belly jiggling slightly, "Now THIS is what I call a Christmas tradition."

But how could this be? How could Santa be fishing when he had millions of presents to deliver?

Well, you see, Santa had a secret. A very magical secret.

There was a place beyond time itself, a land so enchanted that even the ticking hands of the biggest grandfather clock could not find it. That place was called Tír na nÓg, and it was where Santa took his most well-kept and well-deserved break.

Because in Tír na nÓg, time stands still.

It was a land of endless green hills and lakes so clear they looked like polished glass. A place where the stars blinked in every color, and reindeer could be seen grazing lazily in golden fields. Santa had discovered it long ago on one of his Christmas Eve journeys, when a particularly strong gust of wind had blown his sleigh off course. He had landed in a meadow unlike any he had ever seen, and when he checked his watch... time had stopped.

Since then, every Christmas Eve, before his long night of gift-giving began, he made a quick trip to Tír na nÓg to cast a fishing line, let his mind drift, and simply enjoy the moment. Because in this place, he could relax without falling behind.

"Some people need milk and cookies," Santa chuckled to himself, pulling on his fishing line. "I just need a little quiet time before I squeeze down all those chimneys."

As he sat there, a small ripple appeared on the water, and then plop! Something tugged at his line.

"Oooh, what have we got here?" Santa grinned, reeling it in.

But instead of a fish, he pulled up a tiny glowing package.

"Ah-ha! My Christmas deliveries are already finding their way to me," he laughed.

For you see, even in a land where time didn't move, magic still knew its way home. Santa had arranged it so that, while he fished, his elves back at the North Pole could send him last-minute packages through the lake. They would bob to the surface, one by one, ready for delivery.

He carefully placed the tiny gift in his satchel, tipped his hat, and stretched.

"Well, that's enough fishing for now," he said, standing up and dusting off his vest. "Time to get back to work… not that time even exists here."

With a wink to the moon, a nod to the sun, and a twinkle in his eye, Santa climbed into his sleigh, where his reindeer had been patiently waiting.

Whoosh!

With a gust of wind, the sleigh soared high into the sky, leaving behind only the gentle ripple of the lake and the glowing magic of Christmas.

Back in their beds, children dreamed of presents, unaware that Santa had taken his last moment of rest before his grand adventure. And so, as the night stretched on and the stockings filled, the stars above twinkled in the soft light of both the moon and sun, shining down on a magical world that few would ever know.

On the farthest edge of the North Pole, past the toy trains and the teddy bear assembly lines, past the candy cane fields and the gingerbread bakery, there is a special little shop. It doesn't shine as brightly as the other workshops. Its roof is a soft blue instead of red and green. The windows glow with a gentle, golden light, not the flashing twinkle of holiday decorations.

This is Santa's Blue Heart Workshop.

Inside, Santa sits in his grand wooden chair, his big boots dusted with frost. His red coat is softer here, more like a warm hug than a parade uniform. A large heart, stitched from fabric as soft as a whisper, rests on his chest. It glows blue—not sad, but deep and full, like the color of a winter sky just before night falls.

SANTA
(his voice kind and low)

Alright, little ones, who needs a gift this year?

Around him, tiny elves climb onto his lap. Their hats flop over their ears as they whisper into his beard.

BUDDY
There's a boy named Oliver, his dad is far away this Christmas,
and his heart is a little heavy.

SANTA
(nods, stroking his whiskers).

Oliver needs a promise gift, a small wooden bird,
so he can hold it close and remember that love flies back home.

BUDDY
(tugging at Santa's sleeve)

There's a lady named Mrs. Thompson.
She used to bake cookies with her granddaughter,
but this year, her kitchen is very quiet.

SANTA
(smiling gently)

Mrs. Thompson needs a memory gift,
a special cookie tin filled with a scent that brings back
warm Christmas mornings.

The elves scurry to work, carefully crafting each present—not with ribbons and bows, but with understanding and care.

BUDDY
Santa there's a man named James.
He doesn't have anyone to sit with on Christmas Eve.
He watches the snow, but no one comes to visit.

Santa's blue heart glows a little brighter.

SANTA
James needs a kindness gift, a letter, written by someone
who understands what it feels like to wait.

He places a feathered pen in the elf's tiny hands.

SANTA (cont.)
Write to him. Tell him he's seen.
That will be his Christmas magic.

One by one, the special gifts are wrapped—not in shiny paper, but in warmth and love.

As the workshop fills with soft candlelight, Santa leans back in his chair. He watches the elves work, carefully shaping each package. He knows that Christmas is not just about toys and candy canes. It is also about the quiet things—the blue hearts that need a little extra light.

SANTA (cont.)
(whispering, placing a hand over the glowing heart on his chest)

Good luck, my dear ones,
may your gifts bring warmth where it is needed most.

And somewhere, far away, a boy holds a small wooden bird. A woman lifts the lid of an old cookie tin and smiles. A lonely man opens a letter and, for the first time in a long while, does not feel quite so alone.

Santa's Blue Heart Workshop has worked its magic once again.

SANTA (cont.)
Goodnight, sleepy little dreamers.
And remember—sometimes,
the best gifts cannot be seen, only felt.

In the quiet stillness of the North Pole, while the elves packed their final toys and the reindeer stretched their legs before the long journey, Santa Claus stood before his easel. His red velvet coat hung on a hook nearby, and instead, he wore an old woolen sweater, dusted with paint splatters from years of secret work.

Not many knew this, but Santa was a painter. Not just any painter, but the greatest artist of Christmas itself. His paintings weren't for sale or display; they weren't tucked away in a gallery. No, Santa painted Christmas itself—the spirit, the joy, the warmth of kindness that filled homes and hearts each year.

With each stroke of his brush, the canvas came to life. Swirls of golden light, warm fires crackling in living rooms, the twinkle of children's eyes as they crept down the stairs to peek at presents under the tree. He painted the feeling of families hugging after a long time apart, of hands passing warm cups of cocoa, of voices singing carols by candlelight.

A flutter of wings broke his concentration. A tiny elf, no taller than a candle, hovered beside him, flapping his gossamer wings. In his hands was a fresh-baked cookie, warm and sweet, a gift for Santa.

"Master Claus," the elf said, placing the cookie on the table, "you've been painting all night. Have a bite."

Santa chuckled, his deep belly laugh rolling like thunder softened by snow. "Ah, my dear little friend, I must finish this last stroke before I eat."

As Santa reached for a new color, something extraordinary happened. A golden light shimmered behind him, growing brighter, filling the room with warmth that had nothing to do with the fire.

Santa paused. He knew this light.

He turned, and there, radiant and gentle, stood the spirit of Christmas itself. Some might have seen Mary, others Jesus, or even just a glowing presence of love itself. Santa simply saw the reflection of the love he poured into the world each year, given back to him in its purest form.

The spirit did not speak, but Santa understood. His work was not just about gifts, not just about toys and letters—it was about bringing light to others.

Santa smiled, turned back to his canvas, and with one final stroke, he finished his masterpiece.

It was not a painting of reindeer or snow, nor of elves or chimneys. It was something deeper—a picture of the love that moves unseen through every home on Christmas night.

Santa took a bite of the cookie, sighed with warmth, and knew that, once again, Christmas was ready to begin.

dontevenbelieveinelectrons

In the quiet stillness of Christmas Eve, as the last embers of the fireplace flickered and the house lay wrapped in the hush of midnight, a gentle swirl of light began to shimmer in the living room. It wasn't the glow of the tree or the twinkle of the lights—it was something else, something alive.

Through the swirls and flickers of the night, a figure emerged—red coat dusted in stardust, boots barely touching the floor. A thick white beard framed his face, though it wavered at the edges, dissolving into the air like mist over a winter lake. Santa had arrived, but something was... different. He wasn't stepping out of the chimney. He wasn't coming through the door. He was—flickering.

With a sigh, Santa hoisted his sack over his shoulder, his form shifting slightly, as if he were made of rippling threads of light. He rubbed his temples and muttered to himself, his voice soft but crackling like the air before a snowstorm.

"The kids these days... don't even believe in electrons."

It was true. Kids still loved their Christmas presents, still hung their stockings and left out cookies, but belief? That was slipping away. Fewer and fewer truly believed. And as belief faded, so did something else—something Santa had never quite been able to explain.

It wasn't just Christmas magic—it was physics.

See, Santa didn't travel by sleigh alone. That was just the part people could believe in. The truth was, Santa moved like an electron—everywhere and nowhere, all at once. Scientists might call it quantum tunneling; Santa called it The Christmas Effect. He didn't just fly across the world. He blinked, he shimmered, he danced between the molecules of time itself. That's how he made it to every home, in every country, in just one night.

But here's the thing about electrons—they don't like to be watched. If no one believes in them, they act differently. And Santa? He was beginning to flicker.

He reached into his bag, pulling out a wooden train set for a little boy in the house. His hands wavered, becoming translucent, then solid again. He sighed. "Just a few true believers left. That's all I need."

And then—soft footsteps.

A little girl stood in the doorway, her eyes wide, her breath held tight in her chest. She had seen the cookies vanish from the plate, but more than that, she had seen something incredible—the way Santa moved. Like a dream caught between waking and sleep, like the glow of a candle just before it flickers out.

“Santa?” she whispered.

He turned, smiling warmly, but his outline still wavered. "Ah, little one. You caught me."

She stepped forward. “Why do you look like that?”

Santa knelt, his form stabilizing slightly under the weight of her wonder. "Because belief is a tricky thing," he said. "It's like an electron. You can't always see it, but it's there, making everything work. Without it, lights wouldn't shine, your toys wouldn't run, and, well... I wouldn't be here."

The girl thought for a long moment, then reached out a small hand. Santa hesitated. Would she feel nothing? Would she feel air? But then—her fingers brushed his coat, warm and solid.

"I believe," she whispered.

And suddenly, Santa stood a little taller. His form grew brighter, steadier. He laughed—a deep, rolling ho-ho-ho—and in that moment, something changed.

Outside, the world shimmered. The lights of Christmas trees flickered just a little brighter. The stars above twinkled with extra mischief. And in homes across the world, children stirred in their sleep, smiling, though they did not know why.

Because even if they didn't know it, even if they had never seen him, they believed.

Santa placed a finger to his nose, gave the little girl a wink, and in an instant—blink.

He was gone.

But in the air, just for a moment, a tiny flicker of light remained. A trace of something unseen, something electric. The proof of something wonderful.

And in the morning, when the girl awoke, she found something under the tree—not just her presents, but a tiny silver snowflake, shimmering with a glow that never quite faded.

And she knew.

Santa was real.

And belief? Well, that was the most powerful magic of all.

And so, as you drift to sleep on Christmas Eve, listening to the quiet hum of the world outside, remember: Just because you can't see something, doesn't mean it isn't there.

Santa, electrons, and the magic of Christmas—some things will always be real.

As long as you believe.

MERRY

It was Christmas Eve, and the stars twinkled like tiny candles in the sky. Snowflakes tumbled down from the heavens, landing softly on rooftops, tree branches, and the quiet streets below. It was the perfect night for Santa Claus to do what he did best—deliver joy.

But something was... off.

Deep in the North Pole, Santa stood by his sleigh, holding his giant sack of presents. The reindeer were harnessed, the elves had waved their final goodbyes, and yet—something was missing.

"Ho-ho-ho, let's go!" Santa bellowed, but it sounded... strange. Not quite as jolly as usual.

The head elf, Jingles, scurried up, looking concerned. "Uh, Santa? I don't mean to alarm you, but... I can't quite see you."

Santa blinked. "Can't see me? What do you mean? I'm right here!"

Jingles squinted, then gasped. "You're disappearing! You're turning invisible!"

Santa held up his hands—except they weren't there. He patted his belly, but it was only a faint outline. His red suit, his fluffy beard, even his twinkling eyes... they were all fading like morning mist. Only his giant sack of gifts remained perfectly visible, sitting by his side.

"Oh no," Santa muttered, rubbing his now barely-there face. "How is this happening?"

Jingles flipped open the Naughty and Nice List. "Let's see, let's see... AH-HA! Santa, you've spent your whole life giving gifts, but you've never received one yourself! That must be why you're vanishing. If no one gives to Santa, does Santa even exist?"

Santa stroked his beard—well, what was left of it. "You mean to tell me... I need a Christmas gift?"

Jingles nodded so hard his elf hat nearly flew off. "A gift given from the heart! That's what keeps the Christmas spirit alive—for everyone, even you!"

The elves gasped. The reindeer looked at each other in horror. If Santa disappeared, who would deliver Christmas joy?

Then, out of the crowd, little Snowdrop—a tiny elf no taller than a peppermint stick—stepped forward, holding something behind her back. She took a deep breath and presented Santa with a small, clumsily wrapped box. “Santa, I made this for you. It's... it's nothing big, but I wanted you to have it.”

Santa, now just a whisper of himself, reached out and unwrapped the tiny box. Inside was a single, warm cookie with the words “For Santa” written in icing.
As soon as he saw it, a warmth spread through his body. His fingers reappeared. His round belly returned. His beard fluffed up like fresh snow.

He was back.

“Ho-ho-ho!” Santa laughed, the sound rich and full once more. “Snowdrop, my dear elf, you just saved Christmas!”

The elves cheered, the reindeer stomped their hooves, and Santa wiped a happy tear from his eye. He took a big bite of the cookie, savoring the sweetness.

“Alright, team,” he boomed, swinging his now-visible sack over his shoulder. “Let's get to work! Christmas won't deliver itself!”

And with a twinkle in his eye and a jolly chuckle, Santa climbed into his sleigh, his heart full, his spirit bright, and his presence—fully restored.

And that's why, every Christmas Eve, a little plate of cookies is left out—not just for Santa to eat, but to make sure he never, ever disappears again.

Merry Christmas to all, and to all a visible Santa!

nowthisthetrickypart

The moon hung bright over the quiet town, casting a silver glow over the snowy rooftops. Children lay snug in their beds, dreaming of the wonders Santa would bring, while stockings bulged ever so slightly—ready for the magic to unfold.

High above, on the roof of one cozy little house, Santa Claus stood, brushing a bit of soot off his red coat. His reindeer, nestled on the snowy shingles behind him, looked on with mild concern.

“Alright,” Santa muttered to himself, adjusting his belt. “I worked out with the elves all year for this moment. I've cut back on cookies—mostly. This should be a breeze.”

He peered down at the chimney. It was…well, smaller than expected. A lot smaller. More like a decorative chimney than an actual one.

“Now this,” Santa sighed, “this is the tricky part.”

He tugged at his coat, puffed out his cheeks, and calculated his angle. He could probably make it. He'd just need to pull in his belly at the right moment.

Dasher raised an eyebrow. “You sure about this, boss?”

Santa gave a confident chuckle. “Pfft! Of course. I'm a professional.”

He wiggled his fingers, took a deep breath, and…

WHOOSH!

Down he went.

At first, everything seemed fine—dark, a little dusty, but manageable. Then—THUNK!

Santa's belly wedged itself firmly between the bricks.

“Huh,” he muttered. He gave a little wiggle. Then a bigger wiggle.

Nope.

Outside, Dasher winced. “Uh-oh.”

Inside the house, a tiny mouse scurried out of his hole, blinking at the sight of two very large boots sticking out of the fireplace. “Well, this is new,” the mouse squeaked.

Santa sighed. “Alright, no problem,” he grunted, twisting just a bit. “I’ll just—hoist—myself—out—”

THWUMP!

Instead of going up, Santa dropped straight down and landed in a soft poof of soot on the hearth. He blinked. Looked around.
“Ta-da!” he whispered triumphantly to no one in particular.

With a quick shake of his coat, he dusted himself off and tiptoed toward the Christmas tree. He placed each gift just right, adjusted a candy cane on the stocking for good measure, and gave a little nod of approval.

Then he turned to the fireplace and rubbed his chin.

“Right,” he whispered. “Getting in was one thing. Getting out…well, that’s Future Santa’s problem.”

Up on the roof, Dasher sighed. “I told him that chimney was too small.”

But don’t worry—Santa always finds his way, and by the time morning arrived, all the gifts were in place, the stockings were full, and the only trace of his visit was a single, perfectly round footprint made of soot.

And perhaps, just maybe, a chuckle still echoing through the winter night.

Once upon a time, in the bustling halls of the North Pole, where elves clattered away making toys, wrapping gifts, and testing sleds, there was a tiny creature who didn't quite belong—at least, not officially.

Mortimer the mouse was not an elf. He was small, whiskered, and had a tail that sometimes got tangled in tinsel. But what he lacked in elfish credentials, he made up for in heart. Unlike the elves, who were busy assembling train sets, stitching plush bears, and hammering away at rocking horses, Mortimer had a different skill. He painted.

No one knew how he got there. Maybe he had scurried in one night, looking for crumbs, and had simply never left. Or maybe, just maybe, Christmas magic had called him there. Either way, Mortimer had made himself a little home in a corner of the workshop, where he painted the most beautiful holiday scenes on tiny wooden plaques.

Santa never questioned it. He'd walk by, stroke his beard, and nod approvingly. But the elves? Oh, they were skeptical.

JINGLE
(scoffing)

Are we really letting a mouse handle Christmas gifts?

TINKER
Did you see the last one he did?
It had the Northern Lights! A mouse painted that!

So, despite their doubts, they let him be.

Every night, when the elves finally went to bed, Mortimer would climb up to his little painting station, put on his tiny red Santa hat, and get to work. His tail swayed as he carefully dipped his brush into paint. Stroke by stroke, he brought Christmas to life—snow-covered cottages, reindeer soaring through the sky, a glowing Christmas tree, and Santa himself sneaking presents under the tree.

Then one day, Santa stopped by.

He picked up one of Mortimer's finished paintings and smiled.

SANTA
(holding the tiny masterpiece up to the light)

This, is what Christmas feels like.

And with that, Santa made a very special decision.

That year, for children who might not have much, who maybe didn't have chimneys or trees, Mortimer's paintings were wrapped and placed in their stockings. Each one was a piece of Christmas, painted with love, sent straight from the North Pole.

And so, the little mouse became the official artist of Christmas.

As the years went by, the elves built him a proper workstation, with tiny brushes and even a stool so he wouldn't have to stand on his tail. And to this day, if you ever find a small, hand-painted Christmas ornament tucked into your stocking, you might just be holding a piece of Mortimer's magic.

For at the North Pole, big hearts can fit in the smallest of creatures.

And that, my dear, is the story of the mouse who painted Christmas. Now, close your eyes and dream of snowflakes and twinkling lights, and maybe—just maybe—Mortimer is painting a picture just for you.

It was the coldest night of the year, the kind where the wind nipped at noses and tiny icicles clung to window sills like little frozen fingers. But despite the chill, the world felt warm—because it was Christmas Eve. Deep in the countryside, where the stars hung like lanterns in the dark sky, a small stable stood against the winter wind. It was not much to look at, just rough wooden beams and a thatched roof, but inside, a miracle was about to happen.

Three shepherds, wrapped in wool cloaks, huddled near a fire. They had been watching their sheep in the fields when a dazzling light split the sky, brighter than the moon, brighter than any lantern they had ever seen. It called to them, in a way no voice could—like a whisper in their hearts.

"Come," the star seemed to say. And so, they followed.

Inside the stable, nestled in fresh hay, lay a newborn baby, wrapped in soft cloth. His mother, Mary, cradled him gently, her eyes full of love. Joseph, strong and kind, stood protectively beside them. And just above the manger, where the baby lay, that same star gleamed through the wooden beams, casting a golden glow over everything.

The old shepherd, with a beard as white as the winter frost, fell to his knees. "This child... he is special."

The younger shepherds, eyes wide with wonder, looked upon the scene. They had seen kings in grand palaces, but this—this was something greater. A king, not in a castle, but in a stable. A king, not wrapped in gold, but in love.

Outside, the ox and the donkey stood quietly, as if they, too, understood the miracle before them. Even the animals knew: this was a night like no other.

And then, from the hills beyond, a sound carried through the crisp air—soft at first, like the tinkling of bells, then growing louder, fuller, richer. Voices. Singing. Angels, with wings bright as morning light, filled the sky with their song. "Glory to God in the highest, and on earth, peace, goodwill toward men."

The shepherds' hearts swelled with joy. They had not come bearing treasures, but they had brought their greatest gift—belief. They had come as they were, weary travelers, drawn to the light of hope. And on that quiet, starlit night, in a humble stable, love was born into the world. The baby stirred, his tiny hand reaching out.

And at that moment, every heart, from the hills to the heavens, knew the same truth: Christmas was never about what you had, but about what you gave—love, kindness, and the belief that even in the darkest night, there is always light.

And that, dear children, is what Christmas is all about. Merry Christmas, and to all, a good night.

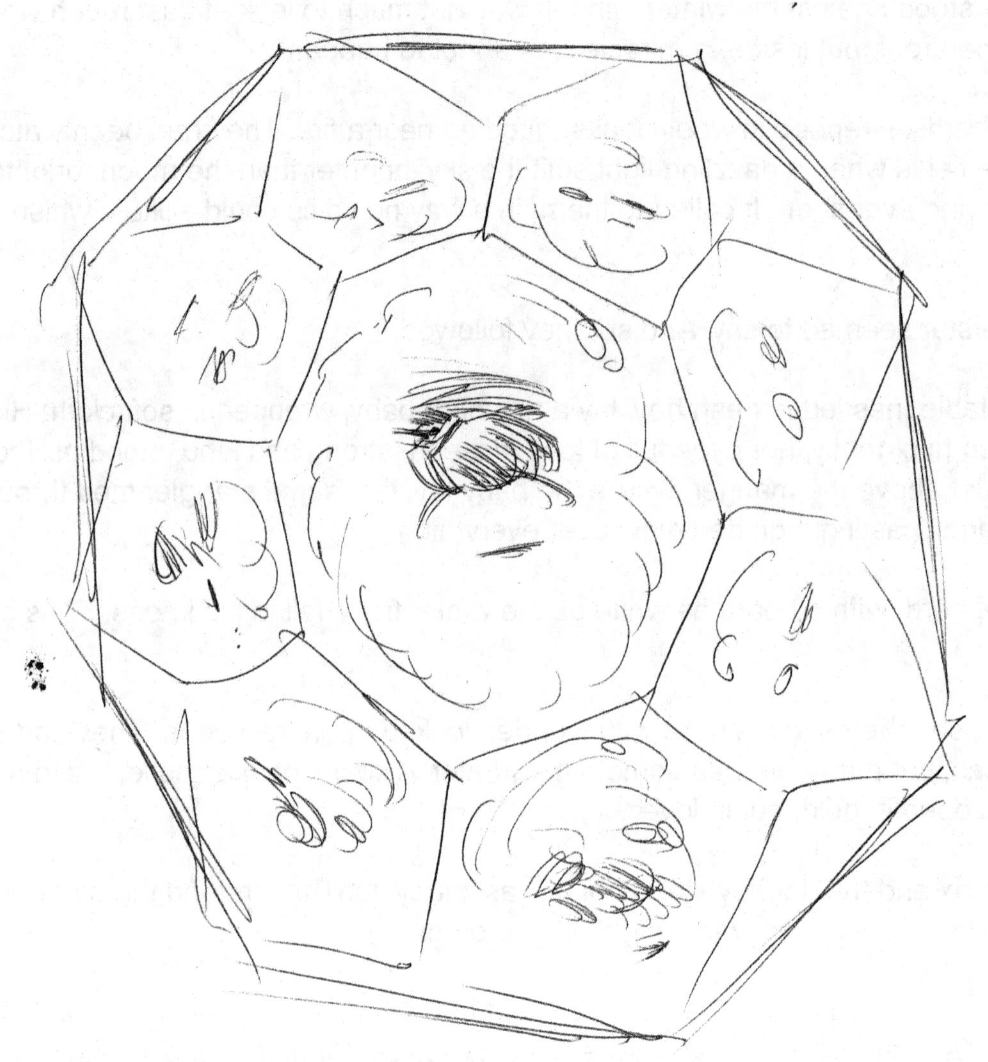

FRACTAL SANTAS

byte size

ENUF 4 all

It was the night before Christmas, and little Oliver lay awake in bed, staring at the ceiling. He had a problem. A big problem. A mathematical problem.

OLIVER
(muttering)

There's no way.

MOTHER
What's no way, sweetheart?"

OLIVER
(sitting up)

There's no way Santa can visit every house in one night.
I did the math. There are over a billion kids in the world.
Even if Santa had a super-fast sleigh,
he'd need to visit thousands of houses per second!
He crossed his arms. It doesn't add up.

MOTHER
(chuckling)

Ah, so you're ready for the truth?

OLIVER
There's a truth?

MOTHER
Of course! See, Santa doesn't work alone. He uses Fractal Santa.

OLIVER
Fractal what now?

MOTHER
Fractal Santa. Santa Claus isn't just one person.
He divides into smaller Santas—perfect copies of himself—over and over again,
like snowflakes splitting into tiny patterns."

OLIVER
Like… infinite tiny Santas?

MOTHER
Exactly! Have you ever looked at a snowflake up close?
It's made of repeating shapes, all part of a bigger pattern.

Oliver nodded slowly. He had seen that before.

MOTHER
Santa does the same thing! As he flies through the sky, he splits into millions of identical versions of himself, each one delivering presents to a different house. And then those Santas split again, over and over, in a perfect fractal pattern!

OLIVER
Whoa! That means… there are infinite Santas on Christmas Eve?

MOTHER
Well, not infinite, but just enough to make sure every kid in the world gets their gifts on time.

Oliver flopped back onto his bed, staring at the ceiling again—but this time, in awe.

OLIVER
That… actually makes sense.

His mom kissed his forehead.

MOTHER
Goodnight, sweetheart. And remember, Fractal Santa is always watching.

OLIVER
Wait, what?

But his mom just winked and turned off the light. Outside, the stars twinkled, and somewhere in the sky, a single Santa Claus soared through the clouds. And then—

Pop!

He split into two!

Then four!

Then eight!

Then a thousand!

And Christmas magic carried on, just like it always had.
And that, my friend, is how Fractal Santa delivers presents to every house in one night.

Now go to sleep before Santa splits into enough copies to see you still awake!

XMAS
Spirit
VIVAS
FUDGE

It was a cold, crisp evening at the North Pole, and the elves had just finished their final preparations for Christmas Eve. Stockings were lined up, gifts were wrapped, and reindeer hooves were freshly polished. Everything was ready. But deep inside Santa's workshop, an important ritual had yet to begin.

At the very center of the great wooden table, among the toy blueprints and cookie crumbs, sat the box.

Not just any box—Viva's Fudge.

Santa cracked his knuckles, adjusted his spectacles, and let out a deep sigh. "Alright," he murmured, lifting the lid carefully.

A warm, rich aroma filled the air, swirling with hints of cocoa, caramel, and just the faintest touch of peppermint. It was the smell of Christmas.

The elves stopped what they were doing. A few reindeer poked their heads through the workshop windows, their noses twitching. Even the wind outside seemed to pause, as if leaning in to catch a whiff.

Santa reached in and pulled out a small, perfectly cut square of fudge. It was dense, dark, and topped with just the right amount of sea salt—exactly how his mother had made it when he was just a little boy at the North Pole.

He smiled, remembering the way she would hum carols as she stirred the thick, bubbling chocolate. "The secret, Nicky," she used to say, tapping his nose with a cocoa-covered spoon, "is love. You put love into something, and it spreads."

Santa took a bite. Warmth. Not just the kind that tickles your tongue, but the kind that fills your chest, spreading through your fingers and toes, until you feel like you've been wrapped in the softest, coziest blanket in the world.

And then… the magic happened.

With a whoosh, a golden light burst from the box, swirling around Santa like a ribbon of cinnamon and joy. His hat lifted, his beard fluttered, and suddenly—he was weightless.

Elves gasped. The reindeer watched in awe as Santa floated upward, his form stretching like a twinkling beam of Christmas light. His laughter rang out—deep, rich, and full—as he became one with the very spirit of Christmas.

It happened every year. The fudge always did this.

With his boots hovering above the workshop floor, Santa let out a hearty chuckle and called down to the elves, "Well, looks like Christmas spirit is in full force!"

The elves cheered. The reindeer nodded knowingly. And as Santa finally floated back down to earth, his feet touching the ground just in time to board his sleigh, the Christmas magic was officially alive and well.

Because Christmas spirit isn't about gifts or ribbons or the latest toy catalog. It starts with something small. A gesture. A kindness. A simple, perfect piece of fudge made with love.

And as long as that love exists… Christmas will always begin at the North Pole.

"...i was waiting for an idea an almost missed it..."

A long, long time ago, before the world knew him as Santa Claus, there was a man named Kris Kringle. He wasn't a legend yet, nor a jolly figure in red, just a man with a long beard and a heart as big as the northern sky. But he had a problem.

He didn't know what to do with his life.

One evening, Kris sat in his favorite old chair, rubbing his hands together, thinking hard. The fire crackled beside him, throwing golden flickers onto the walls. The wind outside howled through the trees, as if whispering ideas to him. But no matter how much he listened, no matter how much he thought, he just couldn't figure out what he was meant to do.

"I was waiting for an idea," he muttered to himself, "and I almost missed it."

He let out a deep sigh, his breath swirling into the cold air. His boots were worn, his coat a little too snug from years of good meals, and his hat flopped over one eye.

Just then, a tiny knock came at his door.

Kris furrowed his brow. He wasn't expecting visitors. He pulled himself out of his chair with a creak and shuffled over to the door, opening it just a crack. The wind rushed in, bringing with it a swirl of snowflakes and a shivering little boy with bright, curious eyes.

"Hello there," Kris said gently. "What brings you out on a night like this?"

The boy, bundled in a patched-up coat and mittens too big for his hands, looked up at him with a hopeful expression.

"Mister," the boy said, his nose pink from the cold, "I heard that you're the kindest man in the village. My sister and I don't have much, but I wanted to give her something special for Christmas. Do you have anything you don't need?"

Kris felt a warmth spread through his chest. He looked around his cozy home, at the little trinkets he had collected over the years. Nothing fancy, nothing grand. But enough.

"Come inside," Kris said, stepping back.

The boy's eyes widened as he was welcomed into the warmth. Kris rummaged through his things, finding a soft scarf, a wooden toy he had whittled long ago, and a small tin of sweet peppermint candies. He tied them up in a cloth bundle and handed them to the boy.

"For your sister," he said with a wink.

The boy's face lit up. "Really? This is for her?"

Kris nodded. "And for you, too. Merry Christmas."

The boy clutched the bundle to his chest and grinned. "Thank you, Mister Kringle! This is the best gift ever!"

And just like that, he was gone, dashing back into the snow with laughter in his voice.

Kris stood in the doorway, watching until the boy disappeared into the night. Something inside him shifted. It was a feeling he had never quite known before—something bigger than himself.

Giving.

Helping.

Making someone's Christmas brighter.

That was it.

Kris Kringle sat back down in his chair, but this time, his heart was full, his mind clear. He knew what he had to do.

From that day forward, Kris Kringle dedicated himself to spreading joy, giving gifts, and making sure no child went without a Christmas surprise. The legend of Santa Claus was born that very night, in the warmth of a humble home, with nothing more than a kind heart and a small act of generosity.

And so, every Christmas Eve, when the snow falls just right and the air smells like pine and peppermint, if you listen closely, you might hear the echo of Kris Kringle's very first Christmas wish:

"Let there be joy for every child."

On a cold winter's night at the North Pole, inside Santa's warm and bustling workshop, there was a little mouse named Mortimer. He wasn't just any mouse—Mortimer was Santa's most trusted cookie companion. Every evening, as the elves packed gifts and reindeer stretched their legs, Mortimer would scurry onto Santa's big, red armchair and wait for the best part of the night—cookie time.

Now, everyone knows that Santa loves cookies. But what they don't know is that for every cookie Santa ate, Mortimer nibbled on a crumb (or two... or three... or maybe a whole cookie when Santa wasn't looking).

"Mortimer," Santa would chuckle, brushing crumbs from his beard, "if you eat any more cookies, you'll be rounder than my belly!"

Mortimer would simply pat his little round belly and sigh happily. "It's for artistic inspiration, Santa," he'd squeak. "How can I paint Christmas if I don't taste Christmas?"

Because, you see, Mortimer wasn't just a cookie enthusiast—he was a painter. And every night, after Santa dozed off by the fire, Mortimer would waddle to his tiny easel and paint pictures of Christmas magic. Snow-covered rooftops, glowing fireplaces, twinkling stars—his little mouse paws could capture it all.

One night, after a particularly large feast of peppermint chocolate chip cookies, Mortimer felt especially sleepy. As he dozed off, tummy full and paws dusted with sugar, he dreamed the most wonderful dream.

In his dream, he was floating above Santa's workshop, his round belly turning into a giant ornament in the sky. His paintings came to life below him—elves dancing, reindeer flying, Christmas lights twinkling brighter than ever. And in the middle of it all was Santa, laughing his great, jolly Ho Ho Ho, giving Mortimer a knowing wink.

The next morning, Mortimer woke up with a start. His little mouse bed was covered in cookie crumbs, and his belly felt rounder than ever. But when he looked at his painting from the night before, he gasped—it was his best painting yet!

Santa picked up the tiny canvas, his eyes twinkling. "Mortimer, my friend, this is the spirit of Christmas," he said. "And I think you should give this painting as a gift."

So that year, instead of just making toys, Santa and Mortimer delivered something special—a tiny painting left next to each plate of cookies, a reminder that Christmas wasn't just about gifts, but about dreams, creativity, and the joy of sharing.

And if Mortimer happened to eat a few more cookies along the way... well, let's just say Santa never really minded.

In the northernmost corner of the world, where the snowflakes danced like tiny ballerinas and the chimneys never stopped puffing cozy smoke, Santa's workshop bustled with elves, toys, and the occasional reindeer with an attitude problem. But today was no ordinary day.

Today, royalty had arrived.

The great doors of Santa's workshop creaked open, and a hush fell over the busy elves. Hammers paused mid-air, ribbons hung loosely from half-wrapped presents, and even Santa himself set down his cocoa. A gust of winter wind followed the newcomer inside, and there she stood—a figure of grand regality, wrapped in silk, draped in flowing robes, and crowned with a golden headpiece adorned with intricate dragon designs.

She was Ms. LaRata, the grand Duchess of the Whispering Mouse Dynasty, protector of the Underground Cheese Reserves, and—most importantly—Mortimer's mother.

Mortimer, the newest (and only) rat apprentice in Santa's workshop, swallowed hard. He had been hoping she wouldn't visit.

"Mortimer," Ms. LaRata said with a slow nod, her voice smooth as melted butter. "My child."

"M-Mother," Mortimer squeaked, scurrying to smooth his tiny apron.

Santa, ever the diplomat, rose from his chair, his belly shaking like a bowl full of jelly. "Ms. LaRata! What a delightful surprise!" He extended his mittened hand. She did not take it.

Instead, she delicately brushed imaginary dust from her sleeve and surveyed the workshop. "This is where you've been?" she asked Mortimer, her eyes narrowing at the candy cane-striped chaos around her.

"Yes, Mother!" Mortimer said quickly, his whiskers twitching. "It's... well, it's not the royal palace, but I'm learning so much. Santa's been teaching me how to—"

"Wrap gifts?" Ms. LaRata interrupted, her voice a gentle chime of condescension. "Tie bows? Stuff stockings?"

Santa cleared his throat. "Actually, Mortimer has a knack for miniature dollhouse detailing. He's our finest micro-painter—look at this tiny toy chest he decorated."

He handed her a doll-sized treasure chest with impossibly tiny filigree painted along its edges. It was exquisite.

Ms. LaRata barely glanced at it.

"I had different dreams for you, Mortimer," she said dramatically, one paw placed over her heart. "You were to inherit the Golden Scepter of the Rodent Empire. You were destined for royalty, not..." She waved a paw at the workshop. "Factory work."

"But, Mother!" Mortimer protested. "I love it here! Santa's workshop is magical! And look, they even let me paint the annual Holiday Cloak!"

He gestured to the very garment his mother was wearing—her ornate dress, stitched with a dazzling hand-painted winter scene. A tiny moon reflected over snowy hills, with reindeer prancing in golden thread. Mortimer had worked on it for weeks.

Ms. LaRata raised a slender eyebrow. She had, in fact, noticed the detailed embroidery. And... well, it was quite stunning.

There was a long pause.

"...It will do," she finally said, patting his head lightly with two fingers.

Mortimer exhaled in relief.

Santa, sensing the moment, stepped forward with a twinkle in his eye. "Ms. LaRata, I think you'll find that your son is quite extraordinary. Royalty or not, he belongs here. We don't just need elves to make Christmas happen—we need dreamers, artists, and hearts that believe in something greater than themselves."

Ms. LaRata studied Santa for a long moment. Then, in a rare display of approval, she nodded. "Very well, Santa Claus. My son may remain in your employ. But," she added sharply, "I expect him to be well-fed and properly housed—no tiny elf-sized beds."

Santa chuckled. "He has a proper bunk, I assure you."

"Hmph," Ms. LaRata sniffed. "Very well. But do not let him waste his talent. And for heaven's sake, keep his paws clean."

With that, she turned gracefully, her golden crown glinting in the workshop's candlelight. As she swept out the doors, the elves released a collective breath. The moment she was gone, Mortimer turned to Santa with wide eyes.

"That... actually went better than I expected."

Santa patted him on the back. "She's proud of you, kid."

Mortimer smiled, glancing back at the dress his mother had worn—his painting, displayed like royal armor. Maybe, just maybe, she had noticed after all.

And somewhere beyond the workshop, under the glow of the northern lights, Ms. LaRata walked through the snow, running a paw over the hand-painted design on her royal cloak.

Perhaps, for the first time, she had seen Mortimer's real legacy.

"say
CHEESE"

It was the grand holiday photo day at Santa's workshop, a time-honored tradition where all the elves, reindeer, and of course, Santa himself, gathered to take the official North Pole Christmas picture. This was the photo that would be sent to all the good children, a joyful reminder that Santa and his helpers were hard at work, preparing for the biggest night of the year.

Everything was set. The elves had combed their hair, even though it barely stayed in place under their hats. The reindeer had polished their antlers, though Donner had a rogue twig sticking out of his. Santa had even fluffed his beard extra wide, making him look extra jolly.

The photographer—a well-dressed snowman named Frostwick—adjusted the camera, looking through the lens. "Alright, everyone, on the count of three—one... two... say cheese!"

And then, suddenly, there was no cheese to say. A scurry. A suspiciously delighted snicker.

All heads turned to the side of the room where, in dramatic fashion, Mortimer the rat stood proudly on his hind legs, clutching an enormous wedge of Swiss cheese like it was the North Pole's most valuable treasure. His little nose twitched with glee.

"You called for cheese?" he said, barely containing his laughter. The elves groaned, the reindeer sighed, and Santa just chuckled.

"Mortimer," Santa said, shaking his head, "that was say cheese, not steal cheese."

Mortimer grinned, tilting his head. "Eh, close enough."

The photographer sighed. "Alright, let's try this again. Mortimer, please put the cheese back."

But Mortimer held up a tiny paw. "Wait, wait! One second. This cheese... is a symbol of holiday spirit! Generosity! Dairy-based joy!"

The elves crossed their arms. The reindeer rolled their eyes. Even Santa raised an eyebrow.

"Fine," Mortimer sighed, placing the cheese back on the table. "But admit it, that was funny."

Santa laughed, his belly shaking like a bowl full of jelly. "Alright, I'll give you that one."

The group rearranged themselves, Mortimer nestled between two elves, looking smug.

"Alright, again," Frostwick said, exasperated. "One... two... SAY CHEESE!"

And wouldn't you know it? Right as the flash went off, Mortimer was holding the cheese again, grinning from ear to ear. The official North Pole Christmas photo?

Everyone smiling. Mortimer holding the cheese. Classic Mortimer.

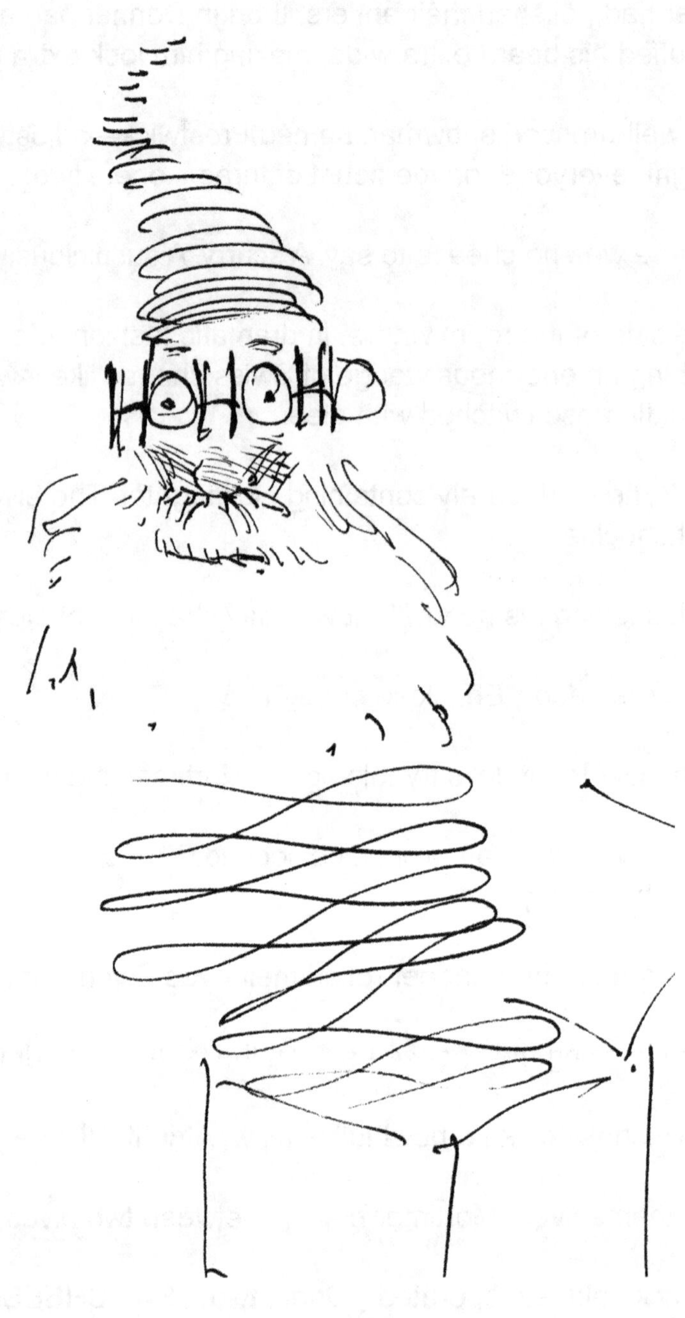

The North Pole workshop was always buzzing with excitement this time of year. Hammers clinked, saws whirred, and the sweet smell of peppermint wafted through the air as elves worked tirelessly on this year's Christmas toys.

But one elf, Jingles, had a brilliant idea. Or at least, he thought it was brilliant.

Jingles was in charge of the "Creative Toy Department," which, if we're being honest, was just a fancy title for "Toys No One Asked For." His job was to invent new things to keep Christmas fresh —because after hundreds of years of making the same teddy bears and toy trains, even Santa liked a little variety.

So this year, Jingles had outdone himself. He sketched, he tinkered, he tested. And finally, on the eve of Christmas Eve, he unveiled his masterpiece to the workshop. He placed it in front of the elves with a proud grin. "Behold! A toy that captures the spirit of Santa in a way that no toy ever has before!" The elves gathered around as Jingles turned the crank.

Clink... clink... clink... The tune of Jingle Bells played softly as the box wound up. And then— POP! Out sprang a spring-loaded Santa head, complete with twirling eyes, a spiraled hat, and oversized glasses that screamed HO-HO-HO! like New Year's Eve in Times Square.

The elves screamed. Peppermint sticks were dropped. A teddy bear lost an arm. Even Mrs. Claus, who had been carrying a fresh batch of cookies, nearly dropped the entire tray.

"Jingles!" Santa bellowed, his beard still trembling from the horrific pop-up. "What in the frozen North is that thing?!"

Jingles cleared his throat. "Uh... it's fun, right? Kids will love it!"

Santa turned to the nearest elf, who was still cowering behind a rocking horse. "Tinsel, do you love it?" Tinsel gulped. "It... um... it makes a strong impression."

Santa sighed. "Jingles, son, I appreciate the effort. But Christmas is about joy, not... well... terrifying children."

Jingles looked down at his invention, now bouncing wildly on its oversized spring. "Maybe the glasses were too much?" Santa rubbed his temples. "Maybe everything was too much."

So, with a heavy heart, Jingles returned the Santa Jack-in-the-Box to the "Do Not Distribute" pile, right next to the "Auto-Gift-Wrapping Machine That Almost Ate an Elf."

But as he walked away, he whispered, "Maybe next year, I'll try Santa with a built-in fog machine..."

And that, my friends, is why you never see a Santa Jack-in-the-Box under the tree.

return to TIRNANOG

The stars shimmered over the vast, endless sky as Santa Claus guided his sleigh toward the one place that no one ever spoke of on Christmas Eve—Tír na nÓg, the land where time stood still.

Most people thought Santa's job was done once he'd finished his last earthly delivery, but there was one final stop left, one that even the elves at the North Pole whispered about in hushed, reverent tones.

It had started long ago when Santa, exhausted from centuries of Christmases, had stumbled upon a peculiar land during a rare moment of leisure. Here, nothing aged—not the trees, not the rivers, and certainly not the kind-hearted souls who called it home. Tír na nÓg was a place untouched by time, where children's laughter echoed through rolling green hills, and the sea glittered like polished glass beneath a moon that never waned.

At first, the residents of Tír na nÓg didn't understand Santa's purpose. They had never known winter, nor the rush of Christmas morning. But when Santa told them of the joy he spread each year, their eyes twinkled with wonder. And so, year after year, the people of Tír na nÓg began to build chimneys—not for warmth, for it was never cold there—but for Santa, so he could bring them the magic of Christmas. Even the tiniest birdhouses had chimneys, just in case a gift might be small enough to fit.

Now, as he arrived once more, Santa grinned at the familiar sight of those impossibly tall, curling chimneys and the little doors left slightly ajar in anticipation. The wind carried the faint scent of honeyed bread, and in the distance, he could hear a lullaby being hummed, welcoming the night.

With a gentle tug on the reins, the reindeer landed on the soft, dew-kissed ground. Santa wasted no time. He moved swiftly, slipping packages into stockings, tucking tiny wooden horses into the nests of songbirds, and leaving just enough magic dust in the air to remind the people that he had been there.

As he placed the last gift beneath a grand, ancient oak, Santa took a deep breath. Here, in Tír na nÓg, there was no rush. No one would wake up older. The gifts would be unwrapped in a time that stretched forever, in a land where Christmas morning was never hurried, never fleeting.

With a final chuckle, Santa climbed back into his sleigh, tipping his hat toward the land that had become his own little secret. The reindeer lifted into the air, and as he disappeared into the night, the words "Return to Tír na nÓg" lingered in the wind like a gentle promise.

For here, in this timeless place, Christmas would never truly end.

XMS. TREE

It was the night before Christmas, and deep in the North Pole, Santa stood in his workshop, surrounded by gifts wrapped in bright red bows, wooden trains, and stuffed teddy bears ready to be sent all over the world. The air smelled of pine and warm gingerbread, and the sound of elves hustling and bustling filled the room. But Santa wasn't watching the toys or the elves. No, his focus was on something much, much smaller.

Before him stood the tiniest Christmas tree he had ever seen. It was barely taller than a teacup, its branches thin and spindly, and it shivered each time a gust of cold air slipped through the window.

Santa stroked his long white beard and sighed. "Oh dear," he murmured, adjusting his half-moon glasses. "You're not much taller than a candy cane, are you?"

The little tree rustled as if it understood. It had been waiting all season to be chosen, to be decorated, to have a place where it belonged. But every time the elves picked trees to send to homes around the world, this little one had been left behind.

Santa knelt down and gave the tree a gentle pat. "Every tree has its purpose," he said with a twinkle in his eye. "And tonight, I think I know exactly where you belong."

With careful hands, he reached into his pocket and pulled out a tiny golden star. It shimmered in the glow of the workshop's twinkling lights, casting little beams of light across the wooden floor.

"Every Christmas tree needs a star," Santa whispered as he placed it carefully at the top.

And then, something magical happened. The little tree, which had seemed so small and frail just moments ago, straightened up. Its branches lifted, its tiny needles sparkled with frost, and the golden star at its tip glowed brighter than any light in the workshop.

Santa smiled warmly. "There now," he said. "Every tree, no matter how small, shines when given a little love."

And with that, he picked up the little tree and carried it outside. Snowflakes danced in the air, and the northern lights painted the sky in waves of green and blue. At the edge of the village, near his very own cozy cabin, Santa found the perfect spot—a place where the little tree could stand tall and proud, lighting the way home for all who traveled through the snowy night.

As Santa stepped back, he gave the tree one last look and chuckled. "Merry Christmas, little one."

And from that night on, long after Christmas had come and gone, the little tree stood tall, its golden star shining brightly, reminding everyone that no matter how small, everyone has their place in the world.

It was the night before Christmas, and all through the world, Santa Claus was hard at work, making his deliveries with a twinkle in his eye and a bounce in his belly. But deep in the North Pole, where the elves were sipping hot cocoa and watching the Christmas tracker, something strange was happening.

One elf named Pip nudged his friend Jingle. "Uh... does Santa look a little... stretched to you?"

Jingle peered at the screen. There, in a rooftop security camera of one particularly science-loving household, Santa Claus was mid-chimney descent—but he wasn't just sliding down. Oh no. He was phasing through the bricks, like a slow-motion magic trick gone wrong.

Back on the roof, Santa felt it too. His jolly belly had started the descent, but his boots were still firmly planted in the chimney. He was... stuck? No, more like... transforming? His beard was already inside the living room, but his arms were still on the outside, reaching for his sack of presents.

"What in the figgy pudding—" Santa muttered, wiggling his fingers, which were now floating somewhere between solid matter and Christmas magic.

Inside, a small boy named Timmy, who had spent the whole year researching Santa's logistics, watched in awe. "Mom! Dad! It's happening! Santa doesn't just go down the chimney—he quantum shifts through it!"

Timmy's parents, who had been trying to convince him that Santa was just a fun story, looked at the glitching red-suited figure in their fireplace and promptly dropped their eggnog.

Meanwhile, Santa, very much aware that he was being witnessed, sighed. "This is why I tell the elves to keep things low-tech."

The magic of Christmas was complicated business, and even Santa didn't always understand it. Some chimneys worked the old-fashioned way—feet first, a little squeeze, and out he popped into the living room. Others, especially in newer homes with modern airflow systems and reinforced linings, required... adjustments.

That's where the phase-shifting came in. A little-known Santa ability that, until now, had never been caught on film. But tonight? Tonight, Santa was being streamed live to the North Pole, and the elves were taking notes.

"Oh, he's definitely shifting between dimensions," said Jingle, scribbling furiously. "This explains how he carries a bag with infinite gifts without breaking his back!"

Pip nodded. "And why he never gets soot on his suit! He doesn't actually touch the chimney walls—he just ghosts through them!"

Back at Timmy's house, Santa finally completed his shift. With a final pop!, he landed squarely on the living room rug, brushing off a few glowing sparks of residual magic.

Timmy gasped. “Santa, that was amazing! You just confirmed every hypothesis I had about interdimensional travel!”

Santa groaned, adjusting his belt. “Ho-ho-hold up, kiddo. You saw that?”

Timmy nodded so fast his glasses almost flew off.

Santa sighed, rubbing his temples. “Great. First, it was NORAD tracking me. Then, kids leaving motion-activated cameras by the fireplace. And now? Chimney livestreams?” He shook his head. “It's like you want me to get caught.”

Timmy shrugged. “I mean… you're kind of a legend.”

Santa sighed again. He pulled a small candy cane from his pocket, waved it over Timmy's forehead, and poof!—instant Christmas amnesia.

Timmy blinked. “Wait… what were we talking about?”

Santa winked. “Nothing, kid. Just remember to leave out the cookies next year. Chocolate chip, preferably.”

And with that, he was off—up the chimney in a blink, magic fully recalibrated, and onto the next house, where no cameras, scientists, or tiny conspiracy theorists were waiting.

Well… at least, he hoped.

The elves back at the North Pole? They were still taking notes.

Deep in the North Pole, where the snowflakes danced like tiny ballerinas in the sky, Santa sat at his grand wooden desk. His coat was dusted with cookie crumbs, his mittens were slightly singed from warming them by the fire, and his eyes twinkled like the Christmas lights children hung in their windows. But tonight, something special was happening—something that no child had ever seen before.

In Santa's mittened hand was The Magic Pen. It was no ordinary pen—oh no! It was long and slender, made from the branch of the oldest Christmas tree in the world. Right in the middle of it was a heart, because everything Santa did came from love.

But the most magical thing about it?

It wrote all by itself.

The elves whispered about it in the workshop. They called it "The Pen That Knows." Because it did—it knew everything.

It knew the children who whispered kind words to their baby brothers.
It knew the ones who shared their toys, even when they really didn't want to.
It also knew when little hands forgot to say please and thank you (but it never held grudges).

And most importantly—it never stopped writing.

Even when Santa dozed off in his chair, his beard slowly rising and falling with each soft snore, the pen kept moving.

Scratch, scratch, scratch.

It was making the list. The real list.

And do you know what? Santa didn't even have to check it twice!

The pen knew who had been naughty, who had been nice, and who had simply had a rough day and deserved another chance. It twirled and spun across the parchment, signing each child's name with a little star beside it—because even the naughtiest children had a little sparkle of good inside them.

"Looks like Sammy learned to apologize today," Santa murmured, peeking at the list.
Scratch scratch—a little gold star appeared.

"And Mia helped her grandma bake cookies," he chuckled.
Scratch scratch—a snowflake doodle danced onto the paper.

"Oh dear," Santa sighed, seeing a name that didn't have a star yet. But before he could worry—
Scratch scratch—the pen suddenly added one.

Santa blinked. "What's this?"
The pen had written:
Sometimes, kindness just takes a little longer to bloom.

Santa leaned back, stroking his beard, then smiled. "Well, the pen always knows."

With a yawn, he leaned back in his chair, his belly giving a jolly jiggle as he laughed softly. The fire crackled, the elves hummed carols in the distance, and the magic pen kept working, making sure every child in the world had a chance to be seen, to be loved, and to believe in a little Christmas magic.

And as the North Pole slept, the pen kept writing…

And writing…

And writing…

Because Santa always knows.

It was a quiet night at the North Pole, the kind of night where the snowflakes drifted like sleepy feathers and the stars twinkled as if they were winking down at Santa's workshop. Inside, warm candlelight flickered against the wooden walls, casting shadows of elves rushing around with last-minute toy inspections. But in the very heart of the workshop, Santa sat alone at his grand desk, staring at the biggest book in the world—the Naughty and Nice List.

It was tradition. Every Christmas Eve, before he set off on his journey, Santa would go over the list one last time. He would give it a thoughtful stroke of his beard, a twinkle of the eye, and, on rare occasions, a chuckle. But tonight... something was off.

Santa furrowed his bushy brows. Something about the list didn't feel quite right. He adjusted his spectacles, squinting down at the pages. One name, in particular, was smudged, the letters swimming together like they were doing a little dance. "Hmm," Santa muttered. "That's odd."

He reached for his trusty quill—one he had used for centuries, dipped in the finest elf-crafted ink. But before he could lift it, a giant fountain pen—much too big to belong to any of the elves—hovered overhead like a great mysterious moon. Then—PLOP!

A fat drop of ink fell from its tip, splattering directly onto the page. Santa gasped. The elves gasped. Even the reindeer peeking in through the frosted window gasped (though Rudolph let out a small sneeze immediately after).

The ink spread like a mischievous little cloud, covering half the names. Santa scratched his head, blinking at the mess. "Well," he muttered, "this is a pickle." One of the elves, a small jittery fellow named Pip, tugged on his sleeve. "Uh, Santa... is that name under 'Nice' or 'Naughty' now?"

Santa lifted the page, tilting it this way and that, but the ink simply sloshed around, hiding the truth. "I suppose there's only one thing to do," Santa said, stroking his beard. "We'll have to guess." The elves froze. Santa... guessing? That had never happened before.

Pip wrung his tiny hands. "B-but Santa! What if we get it wrong? What if a naughty kid gets a pony? What if a nice kid wakes up to a lump of coal the size of a snowball?" Santa thought for a moment. Then, a slow, warm smile spread across his face.

"Maybe..." he said, "just maybe, everyone deserves a little Christmas magic. Maybe, just for this year, we spread the cheer to everyone." The elves exchanged glances. "Everyone?" Pip whispered.

"Everyone," Santa confirmed with a twinkle in his eye. "Sometimes, even the naughty ones just need a little kindness to turn things around."

With a jolly laugh, he closed the book, shook the remaining ink from his beard, and stood up. The sleigh was waiting. The reindeer were ready. Christmas was here.

And this year, Santa had a feeling... it was going to be the best one yet.

The stars twinkled like tiny lanterns as Santa guided his sleigh through the snowy night. The air was crisp, the sky an inky blue, and below, the rooftops of sleepy little houses sparkled with frost. It was Christmas Eve, the most magical night of the year.

But something felt… different.

Santa adjusted his thick red coat and peered down at his reindeer. He listened carefully, expecting to hear their usual merry jingling and the soft whoosh of their hooves through the air. But instead of the familiar chorus of "Ho, Ho, Ho!", there was only silence.

“Dasher?” Santa called. No reply. “Dancer?” Nothing. “Prancer, Vixen? Blitzen? … Rudolph?”

Still, not a single “Ho.” Not even a faint chuckle. Santa stroked his beard, puzzled. "This is strange," he muttered. "It's like someone turned down the Christmas spirit!"

He leaned over his sleigh and took a closer look. That's when he saw it—something truly magical.

Their heads spelled out “HO HO HO.” Santa gasped. "Well, jingle my bells! How long has this been happening?"

He squinted at Dasher, the lead reindeer, whose antlers curled like the letter ‘H.’ Next, Dancer and Prancer, their noses forming round little ‘O’s. And the others—every single one of them—perfectly arranged, unknowingly spelling out the very sound of Christmas!

Santa threw back his head and let out a deep, jolly laugh. "Ho, ho, ho! This is incredible!" The reindeer perked up at his laughter, their ears twitching. "Wait a minute," Santa mused. "That's it! They haven't been hearing my Ho-Ho-Ho!"

He sat up straight in his sleigh, filled his chest with air, and let out the biggest, warmest, jolliest Ho-Ho-Ho of his life.

"HO HO HO!"

Like magic, the reindeer leaped forward, their hooves dancing through the sky. Their bells jingled, their noses glowed, and suddenly, the Christmas spirit was back in full swing. Santa grinned. "Ah-ha! That's the secret! The reindeer don't say Ho-Ho-Ho… they ARE Ho-Ho-Ho!"

With a whoosh! the sleigh soared over the rooftops once more. Santa laughed all the way through the night, delivering gifts, spreading joy, and making sure to always keep his Ho-Ho-Ho loud and strong. And from that night on, he never forgot the true magic of Christmas: It's not just in the gifts, or the twinkling lights, or even in the snow. The magic is in the laughter.

So, as Santa flew off into the night, he gave one last big Ho-Ho-Ho, and if you listen closely on Christmas Eve, you just might hear it, too.

...HEZ making
A LIST and
✓✓ it TWICE ...
...he KNOWS
when U HAV
BEEN BAD
or good

...HO·HO·HO...

iam not
traveling This year

if U DRINK DONT DRIVE

INT. SANTA'S WORKSHOP - CHRISTMAS EVE NIGHT

The elves scurry in organized chaos. Wrapping paper flies. Candy cane shavings dust the floor. The sleigh is parked outside, freshly waxed, ready to defy physics. Everything is set. Everything is perfect. Except… Santa. Slumped in his chair, red coat unbuttoned, gut hanging out like a half-deflated yoga ball. A can of something suspiciously strong sits in his gloved hand. His beard is slightly… damp.

HEAD ELF (PANICKING)

Santa! The sleigh is ready! The reindeer are strapped in! We just need you to—

SANTA (RAISING A HAND, INTERRUPTING)

Whoa, whoa, whoa, hold on there, you pointy-eared narc! Did you know—did you know—that I have been doing this job for centuries? Do you know how exhausting it is to crawl down chimneys for ungrateful little goblins who leave me—what?—gluten-free cookies?

HEAD ELF

Sir, we really need to get going. The children are counting on you.

SANTA

Oh, I bet they are. You know who else is counting on me? The police.

Santa dramatically points at a nearby poster reading: IF YOU DRINK, DON'T FLY!

SANTA (CONT'D)

I mean, do you have any idea what would happen if I got pulled over tonight? "Sir, do you know why I stopped you?" Uh, yeah, Officer Rudolph, because my sleigh doesn't have a license plate, and also, I just blew a 0.18 on the breathalyzer.

He takes another sip. The elves exchange worried glances.

HEAD ELF

Sir… you really shouldn't drink and sleigh.

SANTA

Oh really? Then WHY is every single house I visit filled with booze? Every year, I find a new bottle waiting for me like some deranged Yelp review for Scotch. "Merry Christmas, Santa! Have a whiskey! Here's a rum! Here's a bourbon from a guy in Kentucky who moonshines out of his bathtub!" And I drink them! Because I'm polite!

HEAD ELF

Okay, new plan. Maybe we let the reindeer drive?

SANTA

Oh sure! Yeah! Let's put the whole operation in the hooves of Blitzen—who, may I remind you, got his name because he drinks like an unemployed Viking.

Santa takes another sip, waves his hand dismissively.

SANTA (CONT'D)
You know what? Screw it. I'm calling an Uber.

HEAD ELF
You're calling an Uber?

SANTA
Yeah! Yeah, I'll just strap the toy bag to some guy's Prius and tell him to floor it. Boom—problem solved.

HEAD ELF
That is not how Christmas works.

SANTA
Well, neither is a flying deer with a glowing radioactive nose, but here we are.

HEAD ELF
Santa, please. The kids are waiting.

SANTA
You know what? Maybe this is the year they learn something.
You think Christmas just happens? No, no, no. It's fueled by capitalism and stress.
Do you know how much stress I'm under? I have one job,
but it involves billions of houses, and every year the chimneys get smaller because
some hipster architect in Brooklyn decided we don't need fireplaces anymore!

Santa throws his hands in the air, almost knocking over his can. It wobbles. The elves GASP.

HEAD ELF
Santa. Please. Just… drink some coffee, eat a cookie, and get in the sleigh.

SANTA (SIGHING)
Fine. But if I get pulled over, I'm blaming the reindeer.

Santa dramatically stumbles toward the sleigh, grumbling. The elves breathe a sigh of relief as he hoists himself up. Just as they think they're safe, Santa suddenly sits up straight, eyes wide.

SANTA (PANICKING)
Wait. Did I leave my sack at the bar?

(FADE TO BLACK.)

Don't drink and fly. Not even if you're Santa.

And that's how Santa learned the true meaning of designated drivers.

HEZMAKİNALİST...

On the coldest, darkest nights of December, when the wind howls through the chimneys and the snow swirls like ghosts through the streets, a very special list is being made.

You may think Santa is the only one keeping track of who has been good and who has been bad—but that's only half the story. Because for every Christmas wish granted, every bright-eyed child waking up to stockings stuffed with treats and toys, there is another list, kept by someone much, much older than Santa.

His name has been lost to time. Some call him The List Keeper. Others whisper that he is the one who writes down names that Santa refuses to touch. And tonight, under the flickering light of a candle, he is working.

Dressed in a deep, black coat that seems to drink in all the warmth of the world, the List Keeper sits hunched over a massive, yellowed scroll. His face, hidden behind cracked sunglasses, tilts toward the paper as his bony fingers scratch and scribble. His quill, long and sharp like a crow's feather, drips ink so dark it looks like it was stolen from the shadows themselves.

Scratch. Scratch. Scratch. Another name. And another. And another.

Unlike Santa, the List Keeper does not need letters. He does not need cookies. He does not need milk. He simply knows. The moment a child snatches a toy from their sibling—scratch, the name appears. When a boy tells a lie—scratch, another one goes down. When a girl breaks a promise—scratch, scratch, scratch.

And what does he do with this list? Well, no one truly knows. Some say he delivers empty boxes wrapped in silence. Others believe he leaves footprints in the snow, watching, waiting for children to turn around—only to vanish the moment they look. And some whisper that he does not deliver anything at all, but instead, takes things away.

Toys? Perhaps. Candy? Maybe.

But the very worst children, the ones who spend their whole year ignoring kindness and spreading cruelty—they say the List Keeper takes something far more precious: their Christmas spirit.

So, as you curl up in bed tonight, with the twinkle of Christmas lights glowing softly and the scent of pine filling the air, ask yourself—

Did you share this year? Did you help others? Did you choose kindness, even when it was hard?

Because if you didn't... somewhere, in the dark corners of the North Pole, under the oldest fir tree that no one speaks of, the List Keeper is scratching your name down right now.

And once your name is on his list... well, let's just hope you have a chance to make it right before Christmas morning.

One chilly evening in the North Pole, Santa stood in front of his enormous, ice-carved mirror, stroking his fluffy white beard.

“Hmmm,” he muttered. “Same red suit. Same big boots. Same... jolly roundness.” He sighed. “Maybe it’s time for a change.”

Santa turned to his elves, who were busy wrapping gifts and preparing the sleigh.

“Elves,” he announced, hands on his belly. “I think I need a new look.”

The workshop fell silent. Hammers stopped hammering. Bows remained untied. Even the reindeer poked their heads in through the window.

“A new look?” said Jingles, the smallest elf, tilting his head.

“Like... new boots?” asked Peppermint.

“No,” Santa said. “Something... distinguished. Something that says, ‘I am the magical force behind Christmas. I am elegant. I am refined.’”

The elves exchanged nervous glances. They had always known Santa as the big, cozy, friendly guy in red. But hey, if Santa wanted to feel fancy, who were they to stop him?

So, that night, the elves worked together to create Santa’s new look.

They gave him a long, flowing cloak made of the finest, shimmering fabric. It was dark, mysterious, and trailed behind him like a royal robe.

Then, they placed a top hat on his head—tall and sleek, the kind that made magicians look important.

Finally, Jingles added a stylish cane, in case Santa wanted to twirl it dramatically while making an entrance.

Santa stepped in front of the mirror and gasped.

“Oh ho HO! Look at me! I look... magnificent!”

With a dramatic swirl of his cloak, he turned to face the elves, who were all staring at him, wide-eyed.

Then, one elf snorted.

Then another giggled.

And before Santa could say a word, the entire workshop burst into laughter.

“Santa!” Peppermint cried, wiping a tear. “You look like—like—”

“Like a Christmas magician!” Jingles squeaked.

“Or a very fancy snowman!”

“Or a REINDEER AUCTIONEER!” another elf hollered.

The elves collapsed into a fit of giggles, rolling on the floor, holding their sides. Even the reindeer outside snorted.

Santa sighed. He looked at himself again. The top hat was a bit much. The cloak did make him look like he belonged at a penguin ballroom.

Maybe... just maybe... the big red suit wasn’t so bad after all.

With a chuckle, Santa plopped the top hat onto Jingles' tiny head.

“Alright, alright,” he said. “Back to the red suit.”

The elves cheered.

Santa smiled as he pulled on his cozy red coat, tied his big black belt, and looked at himself in the mirror. Jolly, warm, and magical.

Yeah. This was the Santa everyone knew and loved.

And that night, as he soared through the skies in his sleigh, he whispered to himself, “Fancy is fun, but Christmas is all about warmth.”

And just like that, Santa Claus was back in style—his style.

It was a cold December night at the North Pole, and the elves were working away, wrapping presents, double-checking the Nice List, and occasionally sneaking bites of gingerbread. Everything was going smoothly—until Santa walked into the workshop... dressed like a bird.

Not just any bird. A majestic, mythical, completely ridiculous bird.

He had stitched together layers of fluffy, feathery fabric, draped a cloak over his shoulders like massive wings, and fashioned a tall, patchwork top hat covered in stars. Instead of boots, he had strapped on some oddly shaped talons made out of candy canes and twine.

The elves blinked in silence. Then, as if on cue, they erupted into laughter.

"Ho ho HO, my good elves!" Santa boomed, flapping his enormous cloak. "Feast your eyes upon... The Birdman of the North Pole!" An elf named Tinker wiped away a tear. "Uh, Santa? Is... everything okay?" Santa grinned, revealing a beak he had glued onto his nose.

"Oh, everything's better than okay, my dear Tinker. It's revolutionary!" He spread his arms. "Why use reindeer when I could fly myself? No more feeding reindeer, no more reindeer strikes, no more 'Rudolph demanding better lighting in the workshop'—just me, soaring through the skies, delivering gifts like an eagle!"

A hush fell over the elves. Then someone snorted. And then—complete, uncontrollable laughter. One elf fell backward into a pile of wrapping paper. Another was laughing so hard he dropped a tray of hot cocoa. Even the reindeer, watching from the stable window, shook their heads.

Santa sighed. "I knew you wouldn't understand." He adjusted his feathery cape. "I'll just have to prove it to you." The elves exchanged nervous glances as Santa climbed onto the roof of the workshop. He stood at the edge, flapped his cloak dramatically, and leaped into the air.

For a brief moment—just a tiny, fleeting moment—it seemed like he was soaring.

Then whoosh! Gravity reminded Santa that he was, in fact, not a bird. With a thud and a very un-Santa-like "oof," he landed in a snowdrift. The elves rushed over, gasping. "Santa! Are you okay?"

Santa groaned, brushing snow off his hat. "Hmmm. Perhaps I should leave the flying to the reindeer."

The elves helped him up, still giggling. Santa dusted off his feathers and smiled.

"Well," he said, "I suppose I could keep the outfit for next year's Christmas party."

The elves cheered. Christmas was saved. The reindeer were still in charge. And the Birdman of the North Pole?

Well, he was officially retired... for now.

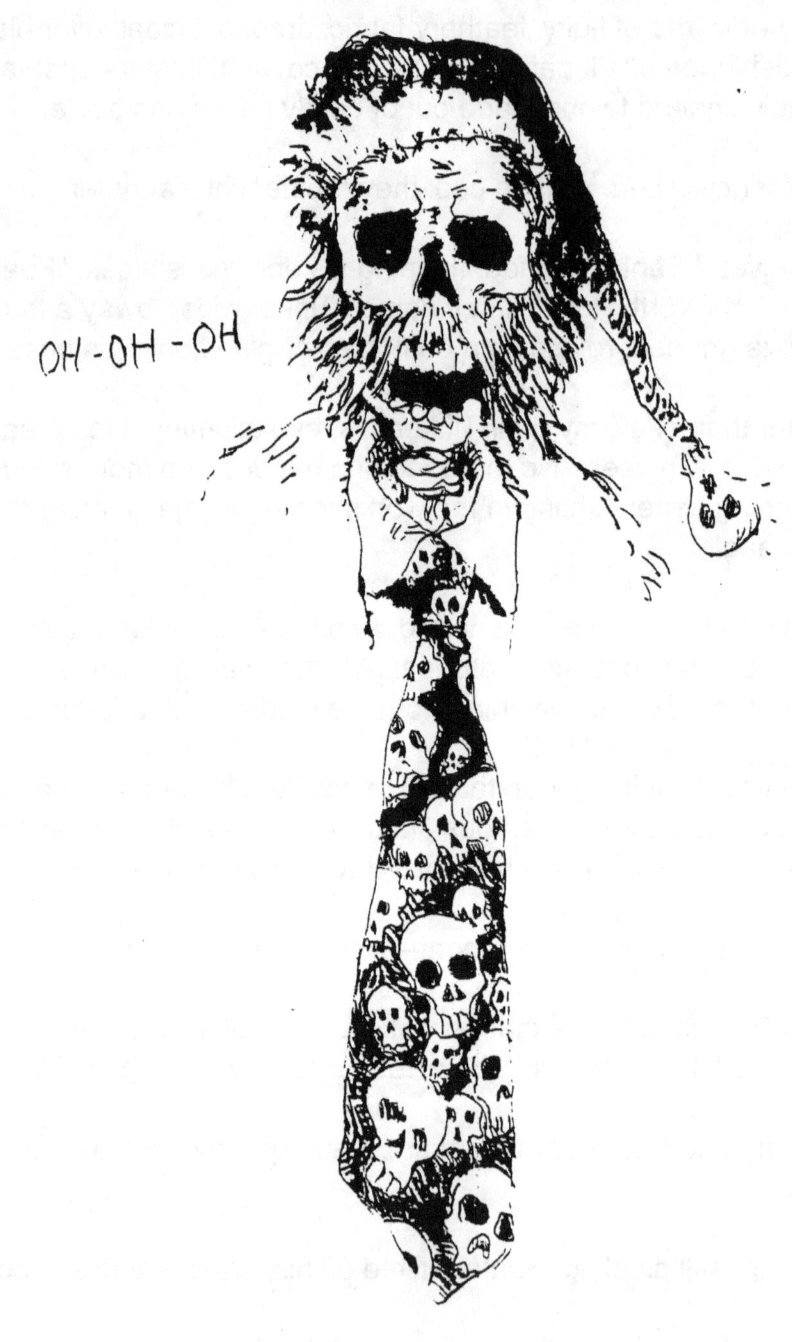
OH-OH-OH

On the coldest Christmas Eve in memory, deep in the frozen North, the wind howled through the trees like a pack of wolves. Children lay nestled in their beds, dreaming of gifts wrapped in silver and gold. But far beyond the reach of twinkling lights and candy cane lanes, in the darkest part of the world, there was something else stirring.

Not all Santas bring joy.

Some bring warnings.

As legend has it, there was once a Santa long forgotten—one who did not jingle with laughter but instead whispered with the wind, rattling through the night like dry bones. His name had been lost to time, but those who dared to remember him called him Hollow Claus.

Hollow Claus did not climb down chimneys. He did not fill stockings with treats or leave presents under the tree. Instead, he came for the wicked. Not just the naughty—no, Hollow Claus had no time for children who refused to eat their vegetables or forgot to make their beds. He was only interested in those who had done something truly wrong.

On this particular Christmas Eve, little Tobias Hartford sat wide-eyed in his bedroom, his breath fogging up the frosty windowpane. He had heard the stories. He had laughed them off, like most children do. But now, something felt different. The night air was too still. The stars, too sharp. And the distant sound of bells… it wasn't jolly. It was slow and hollow, like wind chimes made of bones.

Tobias pulled his blanket tighter around him, but the chill in the air wasn't coming from outside. It was creeping in from under his bed, from the corners of his room, from the very floorboards beneath him.

And then, he heard it.

"Oh-oh-ohhh."

A rasping, breathy whisper. Not laughter, but something worse. It was the sound of air escaping from something that had been sealed too long. The sound of old things waking up.

Tobias dared not move. His heart pounded. And then—he saw it.

A shadow. Not cast by the moon, but something deeper, something that swallowed the light instead of making it. It stretched along his bedroom wall, long and thin, before growing rounder, thicker, until it took the unmistakable shape of a man in a Santa suit.

But this was no jolly old St. Nick.

This Santa was gaunt, his beard brittle and wiry, his suit hanging loosely over his hollow frame. His fingers—long and spindly—curled like talons, and from beneath his tattered hat, black eyes gleamed like empty sockets.

And then, Tobias noticed his tie.

A long, silk tie covered in tiny, grinning skulls.

The sight of it made his stomach turn, but before he could let out a sound, Hollow Claus spoke.

"I have come for you, Tobias Hartford."

The boy's blood ran cold. "W-why?" he stammered, pressing himself against the wall.

Hollow Claus stepped closer. The air in the room grew thick and heavy, like a winter fog creeping into his lungs.

"You know why."

Tobias did know. It was a secret he had kept hidden all year, locked away like a rusty box in the back of his mind. But Hollow Claus knew.

Hollow Claus always knew.

"You took the money, didn't you?" The voice was smooth now, but still dry, like old parchment. "Your mother's savings. A little here. A little there. But you knew it wasn't yours."

Tobias's hands shook. "I—I just wanted a new game. I was going to put it back! I swear!"

A grin curled across the skeletal Santa's face. "Ah. But you didn't."

Tobias opened his mouth to protest, to plead, but he knew it was useless. The stories had warned him—Hollow Claus does not listen to apologies.

Hollow Claus collects.

With one bony hand, he reached into his tattered sack and pulled out a single lump of coal.

But it was no ordinary coal.
It throbbed. Like a living thing. Pulsing, beating, like a second heart in Hollow Claus's palm.

"Take it," he whispered.

Tobias didn't want to. Everything inside him screamed not to. But his fingers moved on their own, drawn to the horrible thing like iron to a magnet.

The moment he touched it, a shiver ran up his spine. The walls around him stretched, twisted, and then—

Darkness.

The next morning, the Hartford family awoke to find Tobias in bed, pale and cold, his hands wrapped around a single lump of coal.

His parents tried to wake him, but Tobias did not stir.

His eyes remained open, staring—forever trapped in the moment he had seen the truth.

That Hollow Claus was real.

And he was still out there, waiting for the next child who thought they could escape the price of their misdeeds.

So remember, children.

Be good.

Or you might hear the whisper of Hollow Claus on Christmas Eve.

"Oh-oh-ohhh."

Once upon a quiet Christmas Eve, a little girl named Molly lay awake in her bed, staring out the window at a moonlit sky. Where she lived, the wind rustled through the pines, and the stars glimmered like tiny lanterns in a frosty sea of night. Though she loved the warmth of carols, candy canes, and bright colored lights, there was something she longed to understand about the holiday. “Is there more to Christmas than presents?” she wondered. And just then, the gentle sound of jingling bells danced on the air outside.

Tiptoeing to the window, Molly glimpsed a figure different from the jolly, laughing Santa she'd always pictured—this Santa sat calmly in a sleigh pulled by patient reindeer, his eyes closed in a serene meditation. He wore a flowing beard and carried a quiet wisdom, like a ripple on a still pond.

Over one eye, Molly could see a faint glowing circle—a perfect, open shape like a rising moon—symbolizing wholeness, clarity, and the endless possibility of imagination. Over the other eye was a darkened circle, swirling with glimpses of Santa in his sleigh, him running over rooftops with a sack of toys, and holiday hustle. It was as if two sides of Santa existed at once: one that celebrated the peace at the heart of the season, and one hard at work delivering gifts to children everywhere.

As Molly pressed her forehead against the frosty glass, Zen Santa slowly opened his eyes. He raised his hand in silent greeting, as if telling her to look within. “Christmas is a time to share your warmth,” a gentle voice seemed to whisper in Molly's mind, “and to remember that real joy comes from stillness, kindness, and love.”

In that magical moment, she felt a peaceful hush fill her heart. Her worries melted like snowflakes on the tip of her tongue, and she realized that she didn't need to do anything special to find the deeper meaning of Christmas. The spirit was there all along, in each act of kindness, each thoughtful moment, and each gentle breath.

Molly returned to bed, pulling the blanket close. A soft peace settled over her, as though she'd been given the perfect gift—a reminder that beneath the bustle of wrapping paper and sugar cookies, there is a quiet holiday harmony that unites everyone.

She drifted off to sleep just as the sleigh soared across the moon, carrying Zen Santa on his silent journey. In her dreams, she heard only the faint echo of his bells, reminding her that the brightest joy shines from a heart at rest.

Late one winter's eve, just as Christmas approached, a curious boy named Oliver peered out his bedroom window. Beyond the soft blanket of snow and rolling hills, he noticed a peculiar shape: a towering tree, its branches twisting and bending like antlers in the wind. At its trunk stood a small carriage house, where a row of stables glowed with a gentle light.

Oliver had heard rumors that this was where Santa's reindeer rested between magical flights. Each December, children all around whispered stories of wondrous hoofbeats echoing at night, of gentle nickers and sparkling bells hidden behind the carriage house door. Oliver wanted to know if it was all true, so with a playful spirit and a coat hastily thrown on, he tiptoed out into the moonlit world.

When he reached the towering tree, Oliver stared up at its broad trunk and lofty branches. The tree almost seemed alive—its limbs shaped like a reindeer's head, gently swaying in the frosty breeze. Above him, its topmost twigs brushed the night sky like the prongs of a pair of mighty antlers. A hush fell all around.

That was when he heard a soft sound—a faint jingling of bells. He looked toward the carriage house, and for a moment, he saw the silhouettes of lively reindeer munching on hay, their breath rising in clouds. The place felt warm and peaceful, as though it were a secret corner of the North Pole that had drifted into his own backyard.

Oliver approached the stable door. It was slightly ajar, and he could see twinkling strings of lights inside. But before he could venture in, an owl hooted from the branches of the reindeer tree above. Startled, Oliver backed away. Somehow, he knew he shouldn't disturb Santa's special place. So instead, he sat in the snow, leaned against the sturdy trunk, and quietly listened.

He closed his eyes, feeling the cool bark against his back. In that stillness, Oliver remembered what Christmas was really about: not just the excitement of presents and sleigh bells, but the wonder of sharing peace and magic with others. The old reindeer tree, strong and steady, seemed to remind him that the greatest holiday gift was the love and hope we carry in our hearts.

At last, Oliver rose and brushed the snow off his coat. "Thank you," he whispered to the tree, as though it were a kindly guardian of the Christmas spirit. Then he headed home, giggling at the thought of Santa returning to find his faithful reindeer safe in their cozy stables, napping beneath that mighty, antler-like canopy.

That night, Oliver drifted into a gentle sleep, dreaming of the reindeer tree's branches reaching for the stars. He dreamed of a carriage house filled with friendly snuffles and jingling harness bells—sure signs that Christmas was near. And he dreamed of sharing the season's true enchantment: a heartfelt wonder that no gift box could contain, as boundless as a starry sky and as comforting as a whispered lullaby.

It was nearly midnight when Santa Claus returned to his workshop, wearily settling down after a long evening of delivering presents. Outside, the Northern Lights shimmered in the star-filled sky, and the elves had just started to doze off after a busy night's work.

But as Santa unbuckled his belt and hung his coat, he noticed something amiss: on the bench near the sleigh's harness, there lay one last gift. A small red package, its golden bow glinting under the workshop lights. Santa's eyes widened.

He snatched up the little box and let out a surprised half-laugh, half-sigh, "Ho–oh–ho… Oh dear, I almost left this behind!"

There was no time to hitch the reindeer again—they were already dozing in their stalls, sweetly dreaming of oats and carrots. Santa didn't have the heart to wake them. So, he tucked the present under his arm, grabbed his hat, and set out on foot through the crisp Arctic night.

The snow squeaked under his boots as he trudged onward. A swirl of frosty air danced around him, and tiny snowflakes sprinkled his beard. "Ho–oh–ho… keep going," Santa murmured to himself, a hint of concern in his voice. His steps were quick yet careful in the powdery drifts.

Finally, after what felt like a thousand snowflakes, Santa arrived at a snug little cottage. Its single window glowed with a warm lamplight. He tiptoed up to the front door—quiet as possible—pushing it open just enough to slip inside. On a small table by the fireplace, he placed the last gift of Christmas. It had a simple tag: "For Ellie. With love and wonder."

In that peaceful moment, Santa felt an uplifting warmth in his heart. The child would awaken in the morning, not knowing how that final present arrived, only that Santa had somehow remembered—no gift left behind.

Outside, the stars twinkled like a choir of silver bells as Santa closed the door. He gave a soft, weary smile. Though his "Ho-oh-ho…" sounded a bit tired, it was still laced with gratitude and relief. Another mission accomplished, another child's Christmas saved.

Then, he began the trek back home, the crunch of his footfalls blending with the hush of the winter wind. And as he walked alone beneath the shimmering sky, Santa reflected on the wonder of it all: that even one small act of care could mean the world to somebody else.

When morning came, Ellie found her present waiting in the glow of dawn. She hugged it tight, delighted by the beautiful surprise. Meanwhile, Santa slipped back into his warm workshop, cheeks rosy and heart brimming with holiday cheer. Though it had been the longest night, it was also the most magical. After all, no distance is too far and no hour is too late when there's one last gift to be delivered at Christmastime.

It was Christmas morning at the North Pole, and while children everywhere were just waking to find presents under their trees, Santa and Mrs. Claus were finally getting a chance to celebrate their own special day. After all, the moment Santa returned home from his long sleigh ride, he tucked the reindeer into their cozy stalls and tiptoed into the workshop, where the elves were waiting to greet him with laughter and cheer.

Outside, fresh snow shimmered beneath an Arctic sunrise. Inside, the elves giggled and whispered, gathered around a neatly wrapped package. They had worked for weeks on this special present, and their eyes sparkled as they held it out to Santa and Mrs. Claus.

"You do so much for everyone else," whispered one little elf, hugging Santa's coat, "so we wanted to do something for you, too."

Santa's eyes went wide. "Ho—ho—what's all this?" he exclaimed. Mrs. Claus gave him a playful nudge. "Let's find out, dear."

Gingerly, they tugged at the red ribbon and peeled back the wrapping to reveal a handmade scrapbook, filled with drawings, photos, and heartfelt notes from the elves. Each page celebrated the joy they'd shared together all year long—cocoa parties in the workshop, friendly snowball fights outside, and quiet evenings by the fire when everyone talked about their wishes for the world.

Santa's rosy cheeks grew even rosier as he realized how much love was tucked between those pages. Mrs. Claus smiled so big that her eyes crinkled at the corners. "It's beautiful," she whispered. "Thank you."

Outside, the winter wind whistled, and somewhere in the distance, the reindeer stomped happily in their stalls. Inside, the elves clapped and cheered. Although Santa had just spent the night delivering joy around the globe, now it was his turn to receive a little holiday magic.

As they all gathered for a North Pole breakfast—steaming mugs of hot chocolate and sweet peppermint pancakes—Santa ran his fingers over the scrapbook's cover. "I suppose children do wonder if we have our own Christmas," he said. "Well, the truth is, we do—and it's made all the sweeter by the love we share."

And that's how Santa and Mrs. Claus spent their Christmas morning: surrounded by the warmth of friendship and gratitude, celebrating in the coziest place on Earth. After a night of bringing magic to every child's home, they found their own little bit of magic right at the North Pole.

¿DO YOU HAVE OUR XMAS CATALOGUE?

Long ago, in the earliest days of the North Pole Workshop, Santa and the elves spent countless hours keeping track of children's wishes. They stored lists in boxes, on scrolls, and in stacks of parchment until one day, the workshop overflowed with paper. Santa could hardly find a place to sit without toppling a tower of tattered wish lists! Seeing Santa so flustered, a clever little elf named Violet dreamed up a brilliant idea. "What if we create one book," she suggested, "a special Christmas catalog that could hold all the toys ever made—throughout time?" The other elves giggled. Was that even possible?

Undaunted, Violet set to work folding bits of magical cardstock and muttering secret elf chants. She gathered peppermint ink from candy canes, pressed fresh pine needles for pages, and sprinkled a bit of fairy dust that shimmered like snowflakes. Night after night, she tucked herself away in a corner of the workshop, scribbling, cutting, and gluing. Santa would glance over with a curious twinkle in his eye, wondering what she was creating. At last, Violet placed the book before Santa. It looked like an ordinary catalog, except for a tiny note on the first page that read: Open me with a hopeful heart, And see the world of toys impart.

The moment Santa lifted the cover, a marvelous sight sprang forth. Instead of simple pictures, each page burst with pop-up figures—dolls and trains, kites and rockets, plush teddy bears, and wooden soldiers. Every toy in history danced to life on the pages. The elves gathered around, gasping in delight as gingerbread houses and model railways seemed to appear from nowhere. Santa let out a deep laugh of pure wonder. "Well done, Violet," he exclaimed. "This will help me keep track of every child's wish, no matter how big or small!"

Word of this magical Christmas Catalog spread among the elves. They proudly displayed it on a grand pedestal in the workshop library. From then on, whenever a new toy was invented—be it a brand-new puzzle or a spinning robot—a team of elves would scurry to the catalog. They'd snip and shape, paint and glue, whispering the same fairy dust incantation that Violet first used so long ago. Poof! Another pop-up would unfold in the pages, capturing the new toy in all its splendor.

Year after year, the catalog grew thicker, containing every gift a child could imagine: medieval wooden horses, futuristic spaceship models, you name it! Whenever Santa needed to see what was new (or old), he'd lift the cover and watch as the pages sprang up like tiny stages.

One Christmas Eve, Santa chuckled upon seeing a new page devoted to flying hoverboards, which had been invented only days before. The elves had already tucked them into the catalog! "With this wondrous book," Santa said, "I'll never miss a single wish. We'll always have just the right toy for every good girl and boy!" And so, in a warm nook of the North Pole, the magical Christmas Catalog rests—ready to reveal a pop-up surprise on every page. Thanks to the elves' tireless dedication and the sparkle of fairy dust, it's never out of date, never missing a single wish. All you need is a hopeful heart to watch the toys come alive before your very eyes.

That, dear children, is how the enchanted catalog came to be. And if ever you hear the rustling of paper late at night, it might just be Violet and her friends, quietly adding your wish to the next pop-up page. Then, when Christmas morning comes, Santa knows exactly what to tuck under the tree—no matter how new, or how old, the toy may be.

LOVE

THISISALLUGETHISYEAR

Late one December evening at the North Pole, the workshop bustled with its usual hum. Elves hurried about painting trains, polishing teddy bear noses, and tying ribbons on shiny, new packages. But tonight, there was a hush of curiosity sweeping through the toy factory. Rumor had it that on Santa's personal wish list, written in big, bold letters, was just one word: LOVE.

In his cozy office, Santa sat at a wooden desk with a long roll of parchment. He twirled his pen between his fingers, a thoughtful look in his eyes. "All you get this year... is love," he murmured, reading back the note he'd scribbled. He let out a gentle sigh. Soon, a cluster of elves peeked inside. They were curious—and maybe a little worried. What about the trains and dolls? The action figures and puzzles? Would they no longer be needed? A brave elf named Maple tugged gently at Santa's sleeve. "Santa," she began, her voice quivering slightly, "is the workshop shutting down? How will we send love to the children if we don't make toys?"

Santa smiled warmly. "Oh, Maple. The workshop's not going anywhere. And we'll still make toys. But this year, I want to remind everyone—both here and all over the world—that the greatest gift we have is love. Sometimes, people forget that in all the holiday bustle." His eyes twinkled as he looked at the parchment. "Of course, delivering love might not be as simple as wrapping it up in a box," Santa continued. "But love travels in many ways. It can soar with the reindeer and sleigh, it can pass from heart to heart in a single smile, and yes, it can even be felt from afar, like a warm thought on a cold night."

Maple and the other elves breathed a sigh of relief. They realized that they could keep making toys—only now, every stuffed bear, every colorful kite, and every sparkling doll would also be filled with an extra dose of genuine kindness. And so, the elves went to work, each adding a dash of holiday cheer to every gift. Some whispered little blessings into the seams of plush animals. Others painted secret hearts in places only the children might discover. Each toy became a vessel for love—tangible proof that someone, somewhere, cared deeply for the person who would open that package.

When Christmas Eve arrived, Santa loaded the sleigh with care. Tucked among the wrapped gifts was his real treasure: an invisible bundle of love, big enough to circle the globe. "Ho-ho-ho, my friends," Santa said. "Let's remind the world what this season is truly about." As he guided the reindeer into the starry sky, Santa could almost feel the warm glow of that love dancing around him like fireflies. Below, the elves waved from the workshop steps, beaming with pride at their new mission.

Across the world, children squealed with delight at the toys beneath their trees. But that year, the feeling of warmth and belonging filled each home in a special way, as though love itself had traveled on the winter wind. Some said they felt a tender spark in their hearts the moment they touched their new gift. Others felt it simply from waking up, seeing family and friends, and knowing they mattered.

By Christmas morning, everyone at the North Pole understood: love wasn't replacing the toys—it was the heart behind them. And somehow, with Santa's gentle reminder, that simple truth glowed a little brighter. After all, the greatest gift of the season isn't just something you can wrap up—it's something you carry inside and share all year long.

KRIS KRINGLE

nice shingles

It was the night before Christmas, and the elves were as busy as squirrels gathering nuts. They scurried around the workshop, double-checking Santa's list and making sure every gift was properly wrapped and labeled. The faint sound of bells chimed from the reindeer stables outside, where Dancer and Prancer pawed eagerly at the snow.

Meanwhile, Santa—sometimes known as Kris Kringle—was up on a neighbor's rooftop, about to slip down the chimney with his sack of gifts. He glanced at the neat rows of shingles beneath his black boots, and a mischievous grin spread under his fluffy white beard. "Kringle, shingles. Ha! Nice shingles," he muttered, chuckling at his own rhyme.

Far below in the cozy living room, sleepy children dreamed of candy canes and snowmen. But Santa, who had made it halfway down the chimney, paused—tickled by his little pun. See, most folks only know Santa as the gentle, jolly gift-giver. They don't often see his goofy side, the one that keeps the elves in stitches back at the workshop.

Because every December afternoon, when the toymaking was nearly done, Santa would gather the elves for a quick stand-up routine. He'd try out new jokes about candy canes, nutcrackers, even reindeer puns (which the reindeer themselves pretended not to hear). The elves would clap and giggle, offering Santa polite applause or friendly boos if a joke really missed the mark.

Over the years, Santa learned that laughter was just as important as gifts. Making toys was hard work, and a little silliness went a long way to keep everyone's spirits high. "After all," Santa liked to say, "a 'ho-ho-ho' has to start somewhere!"

So on that starlit rooftop, after admiring the craftsmanship of those shingles, Santa finally slid the rest of the way down the chimney—still snickering at his pun. He set the presents carefully under the tree, patted a sleepy cat that was curled up on the couch, and left behind a twinkling wave of holiday magic.

Outside, as he climbed back onto his sleigh, Santa patted the nearest reindeer on the head and whispered, "They were lovely shingles indeed!" The reindeer just rolled their eyes (they'd heard that joke more than once). But they set off into the night sky all the same, jingling bells on harnesses and flying toward the next chimney—ready for whatever bit of merriment Santa might bring.

And so it goes, every Christmas Eve. Along with all the presents, Santa carries a twinkle in his eye and a pocketful of jokes, sprinkling laughter just as generously as holiday cheer. And the elves? They can't wait to hear his newest zingers when he finally comes back home. After all, a sense of humor is one of the best gifts of all.

Santa's list

High up at the North Pole, in a warm workshop filled with tinkling bells and cocoa-scented air, Santa Claus studied a very special list. He leaned forward, peering closely, his eyes dancing with curiosity and determination. Above him, his hat's tassel curled around the words "Santa's List," as though it had a life of its own.

Every elf in the workshop knew this list was no ordinary piece of paper. In fact, they told stories of its origins by candlelight. Some claimed it was crafted from the first tree grown at the North Pole, so old that its trunk had absorbed centuries of holiday magic. Others whispered that a playful winter spirit gifted Santa a pen that never ran out of ink, one whose tip glowed whenever a child performed an act of kindness—or mischief.

Year after year, the list grew longer and longer. Names appeared in swirling letters whenever Santa jotted them down. But if a child helped a neighbor, or forgave a friend, the pen would sparkle, and a golden star might appear beside their name—signaling extra holiday cheer. And if Santa had a doubt—Was that child truly caring? Did they remember to share?—he'd carefully check the list again. Then, with a knowing smile, he'd give that name a second chance to shine.

That's why folks say Santa checks his list twice—it isn't about punishing the naughty, but about giving everyone an opportunity to show kindness and love. Every child, after all, can grow and learn through the year.

But what about modern times, when kids have social media, online wish lists, and Amazon Prime deliveries? Some wonder: Does Santa's old-fashioned list even matter anymore? Yet in the North Pole workshop, the elves giggle at this question. Because yes—today, children still hope for special surprises under the tree. And each name on the list still reflects a real child out there somewhere in the world, full of dreams and wonder. Whether you post your wish on the internet or whisper it by the fireplace, Santa's magic pen records your hopes and your good deeds all the same.

So while packages and notifications may fly across the internet in a blink, Santa's List remains timeless, ever ready to reflect the good hearts of boys and girls everywhere. Late at night, when the workshop falls quiet and the toy-making pauses, Santa leans over that enchanted parchment again. By the glow of lamplight, his pen flickers whenever a child's kindness brightens someone's day.

And you know what's truly magical? It isn't just the names themselves—it's what they mean: Each one represents a family, a friendship, a possibility. A chance to do better, to be kinder, and to share holiday warmth. That's a spirit no technology can outshine.

And so, if you're ever worried about being on Santa's List, remember: every act of caring can illuminate your name on that glowing roll of parchment. Even now, Santa might be leaning over his desk, hat tassel dancing, pen at the ready, hoping to put a golden star beside your name—one that says, "They remembered to love and share. And that's the greatest gift of all."

Long ago, before Santa Claus became a household name, he was a kindly wanderer known simply as Nicholas. He traveled from village to village, bringing small surprises to anyone in need—a warm blanket for a shivering family, fresh bread for a hungry child, or a playful wooden toy carved by his own hand.

In those early days, Nicholas's deep, gentle voice had a special magic to it. Children would hear him talk and feel safe and loved. One winter night, after Nicholas had just left a bundle of socks by a family's doorstep, he tripped on a patch of ice. As he stumbled, he let out a booming exclamation:

"Ho—oh—ho!"

Strangely, this heartfelt yelp didn't sound sad or angry at all. Instead, it rang through the frosty night like a comforting bell, making everyone around him smile. Some folks who heard it thought it was the wind, but the children knew better. "That's Nicholas," they whispered, giggling.

After that evening, every time Nicholas helped someone—or saw a child's happy face—he would let out his jolly "Ho Ho Ho!" without even meaning to. The curious thing was, whenever he did, people nearby felt their worries lift. It was as though his laughter carried a sprinkle of holiday magic. Soon enough, Nicholas couldn't help himself. If he saw a group of children playing joyfully or spied a grandparent hugging a grandchild, he'd laugh in his ever-growing, ever-glowing way: "Ho Ho Ho!"

Word of his joyful laugh spread far and wide. By the time he settled at the North Pole and became known as Santa Claus, the whole world knew him for that signature chuckle. Parents would say, "Listen for Santa's ho-ho-ho!" and kids would press their ears to doors and windows on Christmas Eve, hoping to catch just one jolly note of his laughter.

But what makes it so special? Over the years, the elves have come to believe that Santa's "Ho Ho Ho" is powered by every kind deed, every moment of gratitude, and every hug or smile he encounters during his travels. Some even claim that each "Ho Ho Ho" carries a little bit of Christmas spirit into every home he visits—helping people feel warm, loved, and never alone.

And so it is that, to this day, Santa's laugh can be heard echoing across rooftops and chimneys on Christmas Eve. It floats into living rooms and mingles with carols, reminding everyone—young and old—that laughter, joy, and kindness are gifts we can all share. Indeed, his mighty "Ho Ho Ho" is more than just a silly sound: it's a reminder that a dash of laughter can brighten the darkest winter night, and that kindness is at the heart of every true holiday wish.

"¡HO-HO-HO?"

In a corner of the North Pole workshop, Santa Claus sat hunched over his big wooden desk, eyes hidden behind round glasses and worry lines wrinkling his brow. A puffy thought bubble hovered above his head, inside it the words "Ho… Ho-Ho?"—as if his usual jolly laughter had stumbled mid-sentence and lost its way. Outside, the elves were busy in the frosty twilight, gathering the last of the presents. Laughter and jingling bells usually filled these halls, but tonight, everyone sensed a softer hush. Something weighed on Santa's mind, and no one quite knew what it was.

At last, a brave young elf named Pip tiptoed in, clearing his throat. "Santa?" he said gently. "Are you feeling okay?" Santa heaved a small sigh, peering at his reflection in the blank parchment before him. "I don't know, Pip," he answered. "My 'Ho Ho Ho' feels…unfinished. The season is nearly here, but my joy just won't come out as easily as usual." Pip rested a comforting hand on Santa's knee. "Is there anything we can do to help?" Santa gazed around the workshop, noticing all the hustle and bustle of the elves and the half-packed gifts ready to go. "It's just that I sense some sadness in the world right now—so many people feeling lonely or rushed, and I wish I had enough time to sit with each of them, to give them warmth and care."

Pip nodded, understanding the heavy heart that comes with such compassion. "I have an idea," he said. "What if we put little reminders of caring in every gift? Something that tells folks they aren't alone." A faint flicker shone in Santa's eyes. "Reminders of caring?" he echoed. Grinning, Pip reached into his pocket and pulled out a small handful of glittering elf dust. "We'll sprinkle a bit of this in each package. It's a dash of holiday spirit, woven with kind thoughts. Whenever someone opens their gift, it'll give them a gentle sense that someone far away is sending them love." Santa's eyes lit up. "That might just lift the spirits of those who need it most."

Before long, a troop of elves joined Pip, bouncing about with tiny scoops of sparkling dust. They carefully placed pinches into each present, humming soft carols. As the workshop came alive with creativity and purpose, Santa felt his heart lighten. The knowledge that every child, every grown-up, and every lonely soul would receive a touch of extra kindness restored his faith in the season.

Suddenly, the words in Santa's thought cloud rearranged themselves:
"Ho—ho—HO!"

A warm, booming chuckle filled the air, echoing off the rafters. The elves cheered, hugging one another. Outside, the reindeer perked up their ears, their bells chiming in excitement—they recognized that trademark laugh. When Pip looked back, Santa was standing tall, eyes smiling with renewed joy. "Thank you," Santa said to the little elf, "and to everyone who came together for this idea. Maybe I can't have tea with every single person out there, but I can still send them my love in every gift."

That night, as Santa loaded his sleigh under the starlit sky, his voice echoed across the quiet snow: "Ho-ho-HO! And to all, a good night!"
People around the world might not realize that their Christmas gifts had just a hint of elf dust inside—but as they unwrapped their presents, many felt a comforting warmth in their hearts. They whispered, "I'm not alone," and at that very moment, Santa's rejuvenated laughter rose again, carrying hope and love through the winter air.

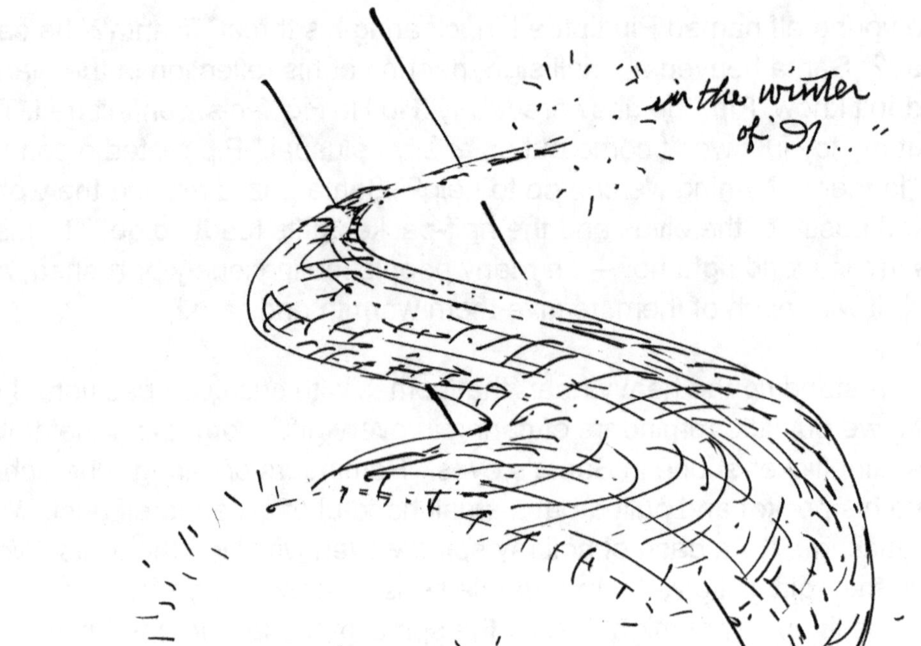

"...in the winter of '91..."

...Santa was in a parallel universe...
...VERY SIMILAR TO EARTH..."

In the winter of 1991—though few on Earth knew it—Santa Claus took a most extraordinary detour. As he soared beyond the North Pole in his sleigh, guided by starlight and the cheerful jingling of bells, he noticed two strange lights dancing in the sky. At first, Santa thought they were just shooting stars, but they gleamed with a peculiar twinkle—like tiny sparks of electricity.

Curious, he guided the reindeer closer. Suddenly, whoosh—the lights zipped around the sleigh, spinning like happy fireflies. In a flash of bright shimmer, Santa felt the world ripple around him. Then, just as quickly, everything went still again—but it all seemed subtly different. The stars overhead looked brighter, and the air felt charged with possibility. "We must be in a parallel universe," Santa said, patting his sleigh. High in the atmosphere, those two strange lights flickered, as if politely waiting for Santa to follow.

"But why bring me here?" Santa wondered aloud. He leaned over the sleigh's side, heart pounding with a mix of wonder and excitement. The lights buzzed and spun around in playful loops, almost as if they were whispering secrets. Then, with a burst of energy, they led the sleigh to a quiet hamlet blanketed in snow. The houses looked like the ones back home, but with roofs that twinkled as though sprinkled with stardust. Santa hopped down from the sleigh to explore. Children slept in their beds, dreaming of bright mornings, unaware that Santa had tumbled into their parallel world. He peered into a window and saw, beneath a charming little tree, a note that read: "Dear Santa (if you exist here), I wish for hope and peace for my family and friends."

Santa's eyes twinkled. "Even in another universe," he mused, "kind wishes look the same. Perhaps I was meant to deliver my holiday spirit wherever it's needed—no matter which world!" And so, gently, quietly, he placed tiny tokens of comfort under that tree: a homemade ornament shaped like a star, plus a small bell that rang with a soft, joyful chime. The two glowing lights pulsed in approval. All through this new, but familiar, realm, Santa left bits of cheer wherever he went. He found children hoping for warmth and laughter, parents longing for peace, and neighbors wishing for friendship. With each gift he left, the air seemed to hum with a radiant energy—the quantum swirl of giving and receiving.

When his sleigh was finally empty, those mysterious lights circled once more, guiding Santa back into the sky. A swirl of sparkles enveloped the reindeer, and in a single brilliant flash—pop—they were back in the skies above Santa's own North Pole. Stars glittered in the same old patterns again, and a gentle hush lay over the workshop. Mrs. Claus found Santa just outside, gazing at the heavens in awe. "You seem different," she said, handing him a cup of hot cocoa.

"Oh, my dear," Santa replied with a wise smile, "I've visited a place both strange and familiar, where children wish for the same joys we do. It seems kindness and hope are universal—truly." And that, the elves say, is how Santa discovered the wonder of parallel worlds. Perhaps he visited to share a bit of holiday spirit beyond our own realm. Or maybe it was just a reminder that no matter where you are—even in another universe—love, hope, and the magic of giving can shine bright.

So, if on a clear winter night you notice two dancing lights overhead, don't be surprised if Santa is near, riding on a cosmic breeze. After all, there's no limit to where he might go, as long as there's someone, somewhere, dreaming of a little more joy in the world.

WINTER time

"makes my hands TWITCH..."

It was the middle of summer at the North Pole—normally a quiet time for Santa and his elves. The snow had melted into shimmering ponds, and the reindeer lounged on green meadows, munching grass instead of carrots. But inside Santa's workshop, something unusual was happening.

There sat Santa, at his big wooden desk, a scribble of plans and doodles spread before him. If you looked closely at his eyes, you'd see a quirky pair of summer sunglasses shaped like the word SOON—reflecting his eager anticipation. And if you listened carefully, you might hear him muttering "Winter… time," through his whiskers, as though chanting a secret wish. You see, winter was still a few months away, but Santa could hardly stand the wait. Every time he thought about swirling snow, crackling fires, and the cozy hush of December nights, his hands began to twitch with excitement. He could practically feel the jingle of bells, the crunch of fresh powder under his boots, and the laughter of children all bundled up in scarves and mittens.

The elves, ever perceptive, noticed Santa's fidgety fingers. One curious elf, named Holly, climbed onto his desk. "Santa," she asked gently, "why do your hands keep twitching? Are you okay?" Santa chuckled, the sound rolling like distant thunder. "I'm fine, Holly," he replied, "I'm just imagining the rush of winter—snow drifting outside the workshop windows, the forging of shiny new toys, the hustle and bustle of wrapping gifts. Even though summer is peaceful, I can't help longing for that magical time."

Holly smiled. "But Santa, we still have plenty to do! We can prepare new toy designs, test out different sleigh improvements, and think of ways to make next Christmas extra special." Santa's eyes gleamed behind his silly SOON glasses. "You're right," he said. "There's always room for creativity, no matter the season. Let's make the most of this warm sunshine while we get ready for the sparkly winter ahead." So, with the help of Holly and the rest of the elves, Santa began a brand-new summertime routine. Each morning, he'd sketch fresh toy ideas on a sunlit porch overlooking the reindeer pasture. His fingers would tingle with excitement each time inspiration struck—a sign of the holiday cheer building within him.

And in the afternoons, he'd gather elves around a splashy little pond to brainstorm. Santa would settle down on a blanket, stroking his beard while the elves tossed around ideas like water balloons—silly and fun, but brimming with possibility. "We'll test them all," he said, "so that when the first snowflake falls, we're ready!" As the sun dipped below the horizon, the North Pole glowed in a gentle twilight. Sometimes, Santa could almost imagine it was the sparkle of early winter, and he'd feel that familiar flutter in his hands. But now, instead of just waiting, he was channeling that excitement into planning, inventing, and spreading a bit of mid-year merriment.

Finally, when the nights grew a little cooler and frost began to lace the windowpanes, Santa's heart started to race. "It's almost here," he whispered in delight, gazing at the sky. Soon, his snow-filled dreams would become reality, and the entire workshop would burst into full holiday mode. But in the meantime, Santa's off-season was hardly dull. Surrounded by sunshine and the laughter of elves, he found new ways to fuel his holiday spirit. And as he tapped his still-twitching fingers on the desk, he grinned. SOON indeed—winter would be here before he knew it, and with it, the joy he'd been dreaming of all summer long.

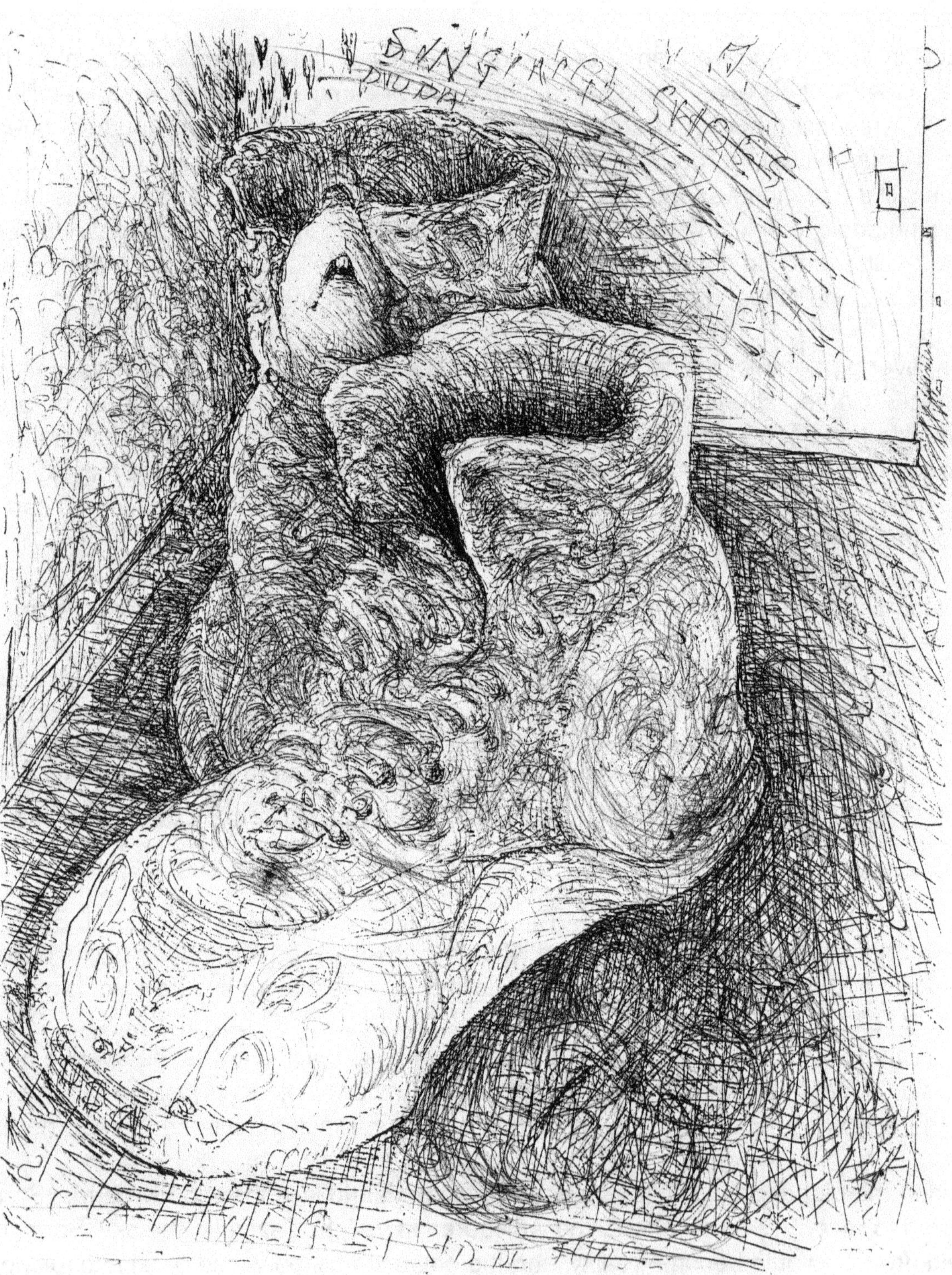

Late one evening at the North Pole, the elves were tidying up the workshop before bedtime, when suddenly—a gentle doo–da… doo–da melody drifted through the quiet halls. An elf named Sparkle froze mid-sweep, ears twitching in wonder.

"Where is that coming from?" she whispered. Carefully following the lilting tune, Sparkle led her fellow elves toward a cluttered workbench. There, beneath a jumble of cloth and ribbon, they uncovered a curious pair of boots. At first glance, they looked like ordinary boots: made from sturdy leather, with little swirls embroidered on the toes. But as soon as Sparkle picked them up, a soft chorus sang out: "Doo–da… doo–da… la–la–la…!" The elves gasped in delight. "They're singing shoes!"

They began poking around the soft lining, searching for hidden speakers or clockwork gears—but found none. Finally, Sparkle noticed a tiny pouch in each shoe. With gentle hands, she opened one and discovered a small, bright-eyed mouse peeking out. "Eep!" squeaked the mouse, blinking at the curious elf. Then, almost shyly, it lifted its tiny whiskered face and resumed singing in a twinkling voice.

"I can't believe it," Sparkle giggled. "The singing is coming straight from this little friend!" Sure enough, each shoe had its own resident mouse, nested comfortably in a cozy pouch—just enough space to breathe and sing without being squished. The elves laughed in amazement. In all their years inventing toys, they'd never seen anything like this.

In the days that followed, Sparkle and the other elves set about making sure the mice had everything they needed. They stitched soft linings inside the boots, placed a little crumb of cheese in each pouch, and even gave the shoes a gentle polish so they'd shine. Then came the big question: "Who should receive these one-of-a-kind singing shoes?"

Santa thought it over. He imagined a child who loved music, who danced through the house creating tunes on anything that could become a drum or flute. Perhaps a child whose greatest wish was to share song and laughter with family and friends. Yes—these singing shoes would be the perfect gift for just such a soul. And so, on Christmas Eve, Santa carefully packed the enchanted boots into his bag, making extra sure the mice inside were snug and calm. The mice peeped a soft lullaby as the sleigh soared into the night sky.

At dawn, a little boy or girl would discover, to their surprise, a pair of unassuming boots beneath the tree. Perhaps they'd slip them on and wonder at the cozy warmth of the lining. And then—ping—they'd hear it: a sweet melody radiating from their own two feet. In time, word spread of the "Singing Shoes Doo–Da," and children everywhere began using their imaginations, wondering what sort of magical friends might be hidden in their own shoes. Of course, no one knows how many pairs the elves might decide to make, nor how many mice are out there practicing their arias. But one thing is certain: if ever you hear a gentle melody while tying your laces, there may just be a tiny friend tucked away, eager to bring a note of wonder into your day.

And that's the story of Santa's singing shoes—reminding us that sometimes, the smallest of companions can fill our world with the biggest, brightest songs.

"YO-HO-HO-HO"

Long ago, before "Yo-ho-ho" became the cry of adventurous pirates, it was a cheerful exclamation shared in the snowy stillness of the North Pole. Back in those early days, Santa Claus—known for his mighty "Ho-ho-ho!"—had a little problem: when excited, he tended to shout so exuberantly that he would sometimes mix up his syllables!

On a brisk December evening, Santa was guiding the reindeer over a large, icy bay, scanning for any floating icebergs. Suddenly, the sleigh caught a gust of wind, nearly tipping Santa and his sack of presents into the frosty waters below. As he struggled to keep them steady, Santa let out a startled but hearty laugh that was neither his usual "Ho-ho-ho!" nor a simple "Ho!" Instead, he bellowed:

"Yo-ho-ho!"

The elves, who were riding along for their first aerial tour, erupted in giggles the moment they heard it. But Santa, always brimming with good humor, simply joined in their laughter. "Well," he said, pulling the sleigh safely upright, "that's a new one!"

In the days that followed, Santa found himself blurting "Yo-ho-ho!" anytime he felt a rush of excitement—be it from tasting fresh-baked cookies or setting a new sled speed record. The elves, tickled by his new catchphrase, quickly adopted it themselves. Soon, the entirety of the North Pole was echoing with jolly "Yo-ho-ho!" every time a bit of merriment or mischief took place.

Now, it so happened that, occasionally, merchants and explorers braved the arctic seas near the North Pole. One season, a scruffy band of sailors ventured closer than usual, hoping to trade supplies. From their ship, these bold visitors heard Santa and the elves practicing winter games on the ice. Above the wintry wind, the sailors caught the booming cry:

"Yo-ho-ho!"

They had never heard such a gleeful shout, and it warmed their spirits despite the biting cold. Intrigued, the sailors returned to their homeland, where they sailed under a captain who yearned for bright, rollicking expressions to inspire his crew. The sailors eagerly shared this new phrase with him: "Yo-ho-ho!" In the cozy ports and taverns along the coast, those words spread like wildfire. Before long, seafarers of all kinds began shouting "Yo-ho-ho!" as they hoisted sails, celebrated good fortune, or toasted friendships at sea. Over time, colorful crews of pirates—the most mischievous sort of sailors—took to the phrase with gusto. After all, the bouncy rhythm matched perfectly with their rollicking songs and rum-soaked shanties.

Little did they know they were borrowing a tradition started by Santa Claus himself, up in the frosty North Pole. And though pirates might sing it by the light of a tropical moon, the spirit of that hearty "Yo-ho-ho!" still carries a touch of Santa's joyful magic—reminding us that a bit of laughter can warm even the coldest nights or roughest seas. So whenever you hear "Yo-ho-ho!" in a pirate song or a story of high seas adventure, remember it all began with one winter's gust and Santa Claus's determined cry to save his sleigh. From snowy drifts to salty decks, that merry exclamation has spread its good cheer far and wide—uniting sailors, pirates, and even reindeer in a single jolly shout.

It was the final hush before the great Christmas Eve journey. Inside a cozy cottage at the North Pole, Santa stood by the crackling fireplace. The warm glow lit up his kindly face, but there was a flicker of excitement in his eyes—like a hidden spark just waiting to burst.

The elves had finished loading the sleigh outside, and the reindeer shifted eagerly in the snow. A gentle snowdrift swirled around the cottage, as though it, too, felt the anticipation.

Suddenly, Santa let out a soft "Ha–ha–ha…" as he thought about the children around the world, soon to awaken to wondrous surprises. With each chuckle, his breath rose like silver fog in the frosty air. Then, in a bright swirl of sparkling wind, Santa felt a tingle course from his boots to the tip of his hat.

Whoosh!

In a dazzling instant, his coat seemed to shimmer with winter magic. His posture straightened, eyes glowed like candlelight, and he became the beloved figure we know so well. The kindliness in his gaze became infinite, and his gentle chuckle grew into a joyous, booming "Ho–Ho–Ho!" that seemed to lift the roof off the cottage.

Time slowed in that single second. The reindeer perked their ears, their bells jingling like chimes in the night. Elves watched in delighted wonder from the windows as the swirl of magic filled the air.

Santa stepped outside, boots crunching in the snow, his sack of gifts bulging with holiday cheer. One glance at the starlit sky, and he climbed into his sleigh. Another rousing "Ho–Ho–Ho!" echoed across the world, and with a playful crack of the reins, the reindeer soared into the crisp night air.

Thus, in the blink of an eye, everyday Santa became the timeless, magical Santa Claus. And so began the grandest ride of the year—delivering love and joy to every waiting heart, carried on the wings of his cheerful laughter.

GLOOM
...in the winter of '91...

Long ago, in the winter of '91, the North Pole fell strangely quiet. Outside, the wind whistled through barren snowdrifts, and inside Santa's workshop, not a single hammer clinked or saw whirred. Day by day, Santa grew more and more glum. His trusty sack, usually bursting with toys, lay empty and still, draped across his workbench like a sad sigh. One frosty morning, an elf named Ember tiptoed over to Santa. She peered at his somber face. "Santa," she asked softly, "why does your sack have no toys this year?" The question made him sigh heavily. He looked down at the limp cloth in his hands.

"I wish I knew," Santa murmured. "We have no materials to make the toys, and the elves—somehow their cheer has dwindled. They've been too tired or worried to craft their usual wonders. It feels like all our magic dust has blown away on a winter wind." Seeing Santa so sad broke Ember's heart. Gathering her courage, she ventured into the workshop where the other elves milled about, listless. "We have to do something," Ember told them. "We've faced challenges before. This time, we just need to find a new way."

The elves glanced around, uncertain. Then an older elf spoke up. "Remember that dusty old trunk in the attic of the workshop? It's said to have emergency stashes of fabric, wood shavings, and maybe even a pinch of magic dust—left by our ancestors for 'dark times.' Could we try there?" With a spark of hope, Ember and a few elves raced to the attic stairs. There, beneath cobwebs and forgotten decorations, they found a faded trunk. Its lid creaked open to reveal scraps of sturdy fabric, wooden blocks, a tin of jingling bells, and—most precious of all—a small pouch marked "Spark of Joy."

Carefully, Ember lifted the pouch. It felt warm in her palm, as though a tiny flame danced inside. Without delay, the elves set to work. They stitched the fabric scraps into patchwork dolls, carved the wooden blocks into miniature houses and reindeer figurines, and fixed little bells onto ribbons. Now and then, Ember sprinkled a glimmer of the Spark of Joy dust. Suddenly, the cloth seemed softer, the bells rang merrier, and the wooden toys gleamed with life. All the while, Santa watched from the doorway, his heavy gloom slowly melting. He approached the worktables, a gentle smile curving his lips. "You did all this with scraps and a bit of dust?" he asked in wonder.

Ember nodded, eyes shining. "We discovered what we already had and used it with heart. That's what makes the magic real, Santa." Santa stepped forward, lifting the toys gently. The moment he touched them, he felt a wave of warmth in his chest—like the first sunrise after a long winter night. His once-empty sack now filled to the brim with these newly made treasures, each one infused with the elves' determination and care. On Christmas Eve, Santa boarded his sleigh with renewed spirit. Though the toys were humble—softly stitched dolls, simple carved animals, jingly little bells—each contained the powerful essence of hope. As he delivered them around the world, children opened their gifts with bright eyes. Something about these handmade wonders glowed in their hands, reminding them that even in hard times, kindness and creativity can spark joy.

From that year on, the winter of '91 became a cherished story at the North Pole, passed down through generations of elves. They called it "The Winter of Gloom that Turned to Glow," and whenever challenges arose, they remembered that a bit of perseverance—and a pinch of warmth—could fill the emptiest sack with the brightest gifts of all.

Every year, just before Christmas, the people of Snowyvale held a one-of-a-kind parade. It wasn't a big, fancy show with elaborate floats—though they had those, too—but the real highlight was a sea of homemade "Santa-on-a-Stick" signs, each one decorated and waved by the town's excited children.

One frosty afternoon, a little girl named Lucy stood on her tiptoes at the end of her driveway. She clutched her own Santa-on-a-Stick sign, which she had painted herself. It had googly eyes and a cotton-ball beard, and it made her giggle every time she wiggled the stick.

Lucy's mom said these signs were a local tradition started long ago. In those days, the roads in Snowyvale were often buried under snowdrifts taller than a full-grown deer! To spread holiday joy, families couldn't rely on big, heavy floats rolling down the street. Instead, they lined up on the sidewalks with homemade cutouts of Santa. When jolly Saint Nick arrived at the end of the parade, he'd look out and see his own smiling face waving back at him from every direction.

As Lucy hopped from foot to foot to keep warm, she spotted Mrs. Jenkins, her neighbor, proudly displaying her Santa sign, which was scribbled on poster board and taped to a broom handle. Down the street, a bunch of Lucy's classmates waved their own Santa cutouts and practiced their holiday songs.

Finally, with a distant rumble of drums and trumpets, the Snowyvale marching band appeared. Their horns shone under the streetlights, and a flurry of glitter fell like snow. Behind them came floats decorated with lights shaped like candy canes, while dancers twirled in fuzzy scarves. Lucy could hardly contain her excitement—Santa would be coming any minute now!

Sure enough, around the corner, a grand sleigh on wheels appeared, drawn by the local volunteers dressed as reindeer. And there, at the helm, was Santa himself, waving a mittened hand and bellowing "Ho-ho-ho!"

"Wave your signs!" the bandleader called, and everyone thrust their Santa-on-a-Stick high in the air. Lucy's little arm stretched as far as it could go. Santa looked out across the crowd, and when he saw a forest of his own cheerful face, he burst into a hearty laugh. He loved the idea of seeing so many "Santas" greeting him.

Lucy felt a warm, tingly excitement in her chest. She knew that, even if the real Santa was busy delivering presents on Christmas Eve, this moment of community, laughter, and tradition was just as magical. It reminded her that celebrating isn't only about decorations or gifts—it's about families and neighbors coming together with bright smiles and sparkling eyes.

And so, year after year, Snowyvale continues the Santa-on-a-Stick Parade. Children pass down the tradition of crafting silly, creative Santa cutouts, and grown-ups keep those warm memories close to their hearts. In each wave of the stick, there is a message of shared holiday spirit—reminding us all that laughter, imagination, and friendly traditions are the real gifts of the season.

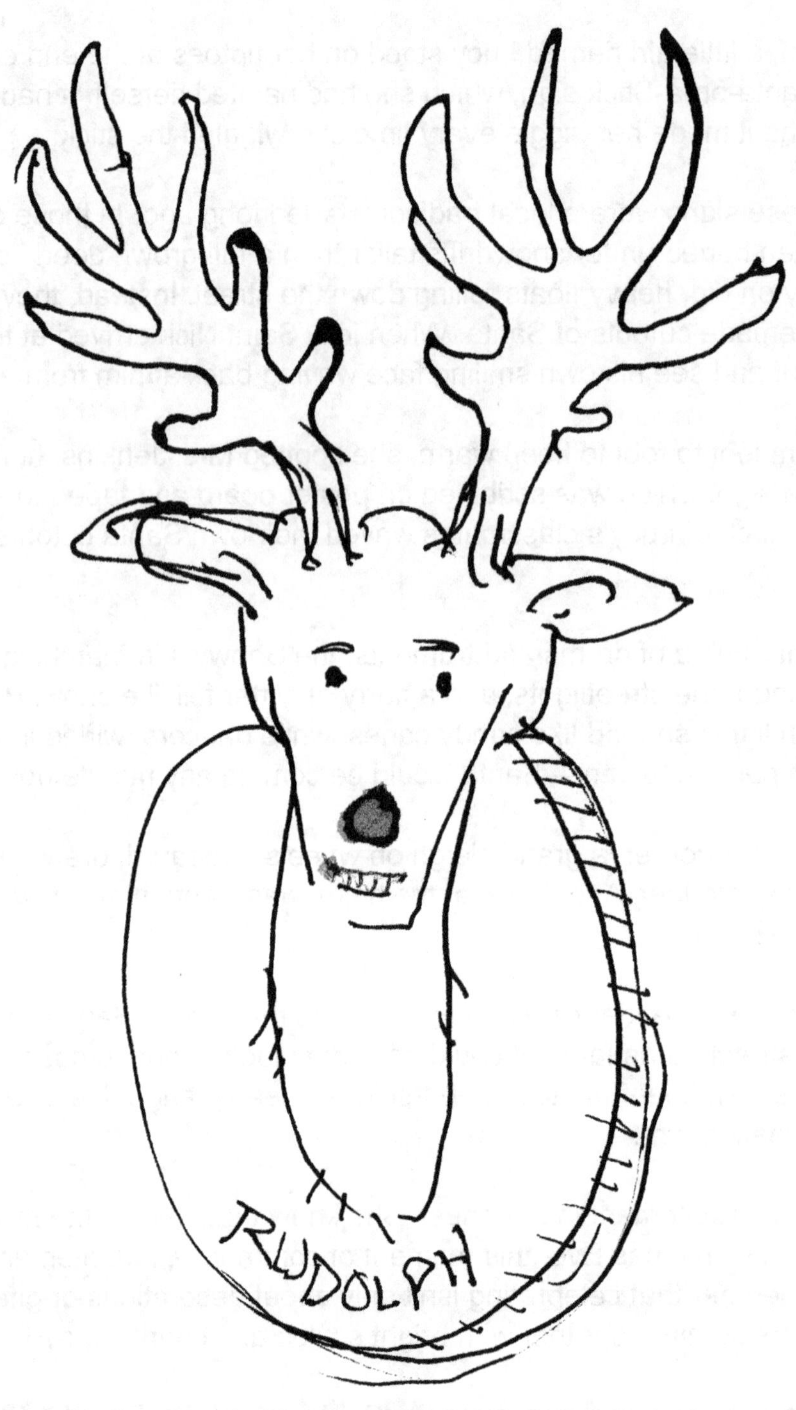
RUDOLPH

Long, long ago at the North Pole, there lived a tiny mouse named Mortimer who dreamed of becoming a great artist. Every evening, while Santa and the elves bustled about the workshop, Mortimer would quietly gather paintbrushes, bits of watercolor, and scraps of paper for his next masterpiece.

One winter morning, Mortimer decided to paint a portrait of Rudolph, the red-nosed reindeer. Rudolph was more than happy to pose, standing tall in his harness as sunlight danced off his shiny red nose. Mortimer squeaked with delight as he captured every twist of Rudolph's antlers and the bright glow of that famous nose. After many hours of careful brushstrokes, Mortimer completed his painting. Eager to show it off, he whisked the canvas into the workshop where Santa and the elves were chatting.

But the moment they saw it, the room fell silent. In Mortimer's painting, Rudolph's body was hidden behind the harness, making him look like a reindeer head mounted on a big wooden plaque! The portrait read "Rudolph" in decorative script around the bottom, just like a trophy. "It's a reindeer trophy!" shouted one elf. "Oh no!" gasped Mrs. Claus. Even Santa's eyes grew wide as he tried to piece together what this strange painting meant.

Rudolph, who was nibbling a carrot nearby, blushed through his bright red nose. "Mortimer!" he exclaimed gently, "I think… you might have forgotten a few important details." Poor Mortimer's whiskers drooped. He peered down at his masterpiece, cheeks turning pink. "Oh dear," he squeaked softly. "I meant to show your harness, Rudolph, but I guess I painted it so large that it hid your body!"

Suddenly, giggles broke out around the workshop. Mrs. Claus let out the first laugh, which made Santa chuckle his hearty "Ho-ho-ho!" Then the elves joined in, and soon everyone was roaring with laughter. Even Rudolph, initially flustered, started to grin. With cheeks still rosy, Mortimer apologized. "I'm so sorry if my painting caused any confusion. I just wanted to highlight Rudolph's antlers and his harness, but now I see I left out the rest of him."

Santa patted Mortimer's tiny shoulder. "No harm done, my friend. We can fix this in no time." Before long, the elves set up an easel and laid out fresh paints. Together, they helped Mortimer add Rudolph's proud chest and strong legs to the canvas. With a few swipes of the brush, the painting became a proper portrait—Rudolph standing tall in his full harness, clearly ready for takeoff.

Rudolph beamed. "That's much better," he said, admiring the updated artwork. "Now the world can see I'm not just a head on a mount!" The workshop filled with applause as Mortimer beamed with pride. And from that day forward, Mortimer was known as "the mouse with the mightiest brush." He had learned that capturing all the important details was key to making art, especially at the North Pole—where reindeer are very much alive, kicking, and getting ready to guide Santa's sleigh.

That night, everyone retired with warm smiles and happy hearts. Mortimer's accidental mix-up had reminded them all that sometimes, mistakes can turn into laughter—and that with a little understanding and a splash of paint, anything can be fixed.

Up in the North Pole, long after the last present had been placed under a tree and the final wink of Santa's sleigh bells had faded into the starry sky, a hush fell over the workshop. Inside, the elves had just finished tidying up the benches and storing the final tools of the season. The grand bustle of Christmas was done.

Standing on a round wooden table in the center of the workshop was a single candle. Its small flame flickered softly, reflecting the twinkle in Santa's tired but happy eyes. This was the Candle of Gratitude—lit every December to guide Santa through the season, and always the last light to be put out on Christmas Eve.

Santa gathered the elves around in a cozy circle. Many were already yawning, their eyes drooping with well-earned exhaustion, but their hearts glowed with the joy of having made so many children happy. With a gentle wave of his hand, Santa invited everyone to sit on the plush cushions scattered around the candle.

"My dear friends," he began, voice rumbling low and warm, "another Christmas journey is complete. Thanks to all your hard work, children across the globe will awaken to magic and surprise. Now, before we rest, let's share one last story—one of hope and rest, of giving and receiving."

In the quiet that followed, Santa's voice wove a familiar lullaby of words:

He spoke of a tiny elf who, on his first day in the workshop, accidentally painted all the toy trains with glow-in-the-dark paint. At first, it seemed like a big mistake—until that night when Santa discovered those glowing trains lighted the path during a particularly foggy delivery. What began as an accident ended up bringing comfort and safety. The elves giggled softly at the memory. He told of a young reindeer, once too shy to speak up, who found her confidence in guiding the sleigh through an unexpected snowstorm. Her gentle heart and keen senses lit the sky far brighter than any lantern. The elves applauded softly, recalling the night they'd watched that reindeer soar with pride.

Finally, Santa spoke of each elf in the circle—of the sparkle they each carried in their own special way. His eyes shone as he thanked them: for their nimble hands, their clever minds, their caring spirits, and for each smile shared in the workshop.

When his last words faded into the silence, Santa reached out to the candle. Its flame glowed more brightly than ever, as if celebrating their togetherness. "Now," he said, "we rest. And tomorrow begins a new day—one of peace, reflection, and well-deserved slumber."

With a soft breath, Santa blew out the Candle of Gratitude. In that gentle darkness, the elves felt a lovely sense of calm, like a soothing blanket settling over their hearts. One by one, they slipped away to their bunks, tiny yawns and murmured goodnights drifting through the corridors.

And so the last light of Christmas Eve disappeared, leaving behind a cozy glow inside every elf and Santa himself—a reminder that even when the candle's flame is gone, the warmth of gratitude lingers on, lighting the way until the next season of magic dawns.

¿WHO WOULDN'T WANT!

a hand drawn self-portrait of santa claus in 1994

Long ago, when the North Pole was abuzz with Christmas preparations, a little mouse named Mortimer scurried to and fro with paint-splattered fur. He was the resident artist—known for his vibrant imagination and gentle persistence. Over time, Mortimer had painted everything from nutcracker designs to wintry murals on the workshop walls, but he always felt there was one project missing. One frosty afternoon, as Santa took a rare break from the toy factory, Mortimer mustered his courage and scurried up onto Santa's workbench. "Santa," he squeaked, nibbling on the tip of his paintbrush, "you've brought so much joy into everyone else's lives. Have you ever thought about painting yourself—a self-portrait, so the world can see how you see you?"

Santa blinked in surprise. It wasn't that he disliked painting—he just never considered it. "Why, Mortimer, I've never taken the time!" he chuckled. "The elves and I stay so busy with toys and gifts... I'm not sure I'd be any good at capturing my own face on canvas." But Mortimer's eyes sparkled with quiet determination. "Please, Santa. I'll help you. Just think: you've been around for so many Christmases, always making others happy. Wouldn't it be nice to create something for yourself, too?"

Santa scratched his snowy beard, his cheeks turning pink. Finally, he gave a nod. "Let's do it, Mortimer. But you'd better guide me." And so began a series of magical painting sessions in the quiet corners of the North Pole. When the elves were busy assembling music boxes or the reindeer were out for their daily flight, Santa and Mortimer slipped away with an easel, brushes, and little pots of colored paint.

At first, Santa struggled—he wasn't quite sure how to transfer that twinkle in his eye or the kindness in his smile onto the canvas. But Mortimer scurried around, dabbing different hues and showing Santa the basics of shading and blending. "Focus on what you feel," Mortimer advised. "After all, your spirit is the most important thing to show!" Gradually, Santa relaxed. He laughed whenever a line came out wonky or a color didn't look right. Each mistake turned into a playful discovery. Little by little, a charming likeness emerged: warm, crinkly eyes, a fluffy beard with glimmers of white and silver, and a gentle curve of a smile that spoke of endless compassion.

By the time the final brushstroke was placed, word had spread among the elves: Santa was creating his very first self-portrait! They gathered around, craning their necks to admire it. Mortimer insisted on framing the portrait. He carved a simple wooden frame, lightly staining it so the grain stood out. Then, in festive lettering, he wrote: "A hand-drawn self-portrait of Santa Claus, 1994." Above it, he added, "Who wouldn't want?"—because in his mind, anyone who cherished Christmas would treasure a peek into Santa's own view of himself.

Finally, Santa hung the painting in a cozy corner of the workshop. Every now and then, when the holiday stress felt overwhelming, he'd glance at that portrait and remember the quiet joy of creating something just for the love of it—and the gratitude he felt for Mortimer, who encouraged him to see his own spirit reflected in art. To this day, if you wander through the North Pole's workshop, you might spot that framed masterpiece: a reminder that even Santa, the busiest gift-giver in the world, once found time to sit down with a brush and a friend, to paint the kindness shining in his own heart. And for Mortimer, that portrait still stands as proof that no dream is too big—or too small—when you have the courage to share it with someone who believes in you.

Late one snowy evening at the North Pole, Santa sat at his old wooden desk with a curious smile on his face. A single candle flickered in the workshop, casting dancing shadows across the walls. Above his head, a thought bubble shimmered with the image of a big, shining eye.

To the elves bustling nearby, it looked as if Santa was deep in thought about the question children everywhere ask: “How does Santa see who’s good or bad?”

In truth, Santa has a very special way of keeping track. It isn’t just about blinking eyeballs—it’s a gentle, magical sense in his heart. Whenever a child does something kind—like sharing a toy, helping a sibling, or giving a friend a hug—Santa feels a warm glow in his chest. You could say it’s a little spark, something like hearing a tiny bell chime.

Likewise, if a child is feeling grumpy or makes a mistake—like saying an unkind word—Santa senses a soft twinge of concern. Not a scary or angry feeling, but more like a gentle tug reminding him to pay attention and send a bit of extra cheer that child’s way, so they can learn and grow from that moment.

Of course, there are so many children in the world that it’s not always easy, even for Santa. Sometimes he feels too many bells at once, or too many twinges, and it all blurs together like a winter storm. On those days, the elves help out by telling him stories about the children’s acts of kindness and honesty. They also remind him that everyone makes mistakes—and Santa knows it isn’t about tallying up ‘naughty vs. nice,’ but helping children find their best selves over time.

That’s why sometimes Santa adjusts his magical sense. If he feels a confused child struggling, he’ll focus on sending them a spark of encouragement. If a child has been especially generous, he’ll smile extra wide, feeling the joy of their good deed. This way, even if Santa can’t literally see every action, he can feel the warmth or sadness traveling through the world—like a soft pulse guiding him to where he’s needed most.

And yes, sometimes Santa may get it a bit wrong—he’s only human (well, mostly!). But that’s why he checks his lists twice, and why he trusts the kindness of parents, teachers, and friends to help guide children along. Santa believes in second chances, in the power of learning from mistakes, and in the truth that nobody’s perfectly good or bad. We’re all on a journey, and the important thing is making the effort to grow kinder each day.

So, next time you wonder how Santa sees you, remember: it’s not just an eye in the sky. It’s a mix of gentle magic and heartfelt hope—an old elf’s understanding that every child deserves patience, support, and a shining chance to do better. And if you ever slip or stray? Santa will still be there, believing in you more than ever, ready to share a twinkle of that North Pole cheer to help you find your way back.

Every Christmas Eve, children imagine Santa Claus flying through the night sky in his sleigh, guided by the soft glow of Rudolph's nose. But what few people realize is that long before he uses reindeer to traverse snowy rooftops, Santa sets out from a quiet pier at the North Pole, on a secret journey across the seas.

It all starts when winter's twilight settles over the Arctic. Tucked by an icy dock sits Santa's special boat—a curious vessel that looks just like his cozy North Pole cottage, except perched on a sturdy hull. Its mast stands tall, draped with a cheerful flag bearing an image of a twinkling star. One frosty morning, as icy water laps at the shore, Santa steps aboard in his plush red coat. Tiny waves ripple around the hull as he checks his compass, which isn't just any compass, but a magical one that orients itself toward good deeds and warm hearts. The elves wave from the pier, their cheeks pink in the brisk polar wind.

"Safe travels!" they call. "We'll see you soon!"

With a creak of the mast and a gentle push, Santa sets sail. Quiet though it may seem, the boat holds a special cargo within its wooden cabin: gift-wrapped presents for children who live near docks and coastlines around the world. Some homes stand on stilts above the water, others cling to rocky shores, and many harbor towns line the coasts with twinkling lights.

Up in the crow's nest, a friendly seagull named Maribel serves as Santa's lookout, squawking whenever she spies a child's cozy lighthouse or a lamplit harbor. At dusk, Santa often hums holiday tunes as he steers the boat through the moonlit sea, guided by shimmering stars above and the gentle lapping of waves against the bow.

When Santa arrives at his first waterfront stop—perhaps a small fishing village—he moors quietly by a wooden dock. With a soft step and a warm grin, he tiptoes onto the shore, carrying packages wrapped in ocean-themed paper. Sometimes, seals peek their heads up from the water, as if to watch Santa's careful footsteps on the slippery rocks.

In each little cove or bay, children sleep snugly, never guessing Santa's boat gently drifts outside in the midnight tide. He leaves gifts by cottage doors—shell-decorated music boxes, cuddly plush sea otters, or a simple stuffed bear wearing a sailor's hat. Then, with a knowing wink, he returns to the boat to continue his voyage.

Now, you might wonder how Santa can reach everyone around the globe in just one night. Well, the same magic that lifts his sleigh also propels this humble boat, creating swift currents and friendly winds. Time itself seems to slow down in the glow of Santa's kindness. By sunrise, he has delivered cheer to countless shores, returning to the North Pole with a heart full of gratitude for every wave and whitecap that guided him safely home.

And so, when you picture Santa on Christmas Eve, don't forget to imagine him sailing quietly under starry skies, the gentle hum of ocean breezes blending with faint jingle bells. After all, joy can arrive by many paths—be it skies, sleigh, or sea. And those who live by the coast might awaken to the faint echo of a festive foghorn, smiling as they realize Santa's seafaring sleigh made its merry stop in the night.

...a running ginger bread man
WAS DIS·CONTINUED..."

Deep within the North Pole workshop, where fragrant cinnamon and peppermint scents often mingle, Santa and his elves once experimented with a brand-new treat: a running gingerbread man modeled after Santa himself, mid-flight on rooftops. Picture a cheerful pastry, complete with a little gingerbread beard, a miniature sack, and icing boots that seemed to dash forward—just like Santa on Christmas Eve.

At first, the elves were thrilled by the idea. They carefully measured spices and dough, rolling out sheets of gingerbread large enough to create a life-sized figure. And sure enough, once the baking was done, the result looked astonishing—like a statue of Santa in cookie form, frozen in that iconic sprint across chimney tops.

But soon, a few problems rose—just like the dough! It broke too easily. Though the elves had used the strongest sugar glazes they could, any jostle caused the gingerbread's limbs to snap. Mortimer the mouse discovered the delicious treat. With his tiny paint-stained whiskers, he'd sneak over and nibble discreetly at the cookie edges whenever no one was looking.
Even the reindeer couldn't resist a midnight snack. Rudolph and friends would wander by, pick up that sweet aroma, and chomp on a cookie foot or an icing mitten. Before long, the once-proud gingerbread man looked more like a half-finished art project, missing a chunk of arm here, part of a beard there. Santa soon realized that despite its charm, the gingerbread Santa was in danger of vanishing piece by piece—and not in the delicious way a typical gingerbread cookie might!

Gathering the elves in the main kitchen one evening, Santa held up what remained of the treat. "My dear friends," he said with a regretful smile, "our running gingerbread man may taste delightful, but it just can't survive a bustling workshop. And honestly, I don't think we can patch it up any more than we have. Let's not keep baking these, or it'll keep disappearing in nibbles!"

A wave of understanding sighs spread among the elves—some a little disappointed, some hungry from the spicy-sweet aroma. Mortimer peered out sheepishly from behind a mixing bowl, crumbs still on his whiskers, squeaking a tiny apology. The reindeer, peeking in the kitchen window, gave wide-eyed, guilty looks, too.

But Santa, ever kind, placed a comforting hand on Mortimer's head. "It was a wonderful idea. Sometimes, though, the best inventions don't last forever. Maybe one day we'll find a way to make a stronger, more nibble-proof gingerbread figure. Until then, we'll stick with smaller cookies that don't tempt our four-legged friends quite as much."

That night, the elves broke the massive gingerbread Santa into shareable pieces, forming a spontaneous holiday feast. They brewed hot cocoa and had a lively cookie party, complete with laughter and carols. The reindeer got their fill of sweet treats, and Mortimer—much to his delight—nibbled to his heart's content without fear of scolding.

And thus, the running gingerbread man was discontinued—but not forgotten. In fact, the memory lived on as one of those whimsical North Pole moments where creativity, fun, and a little chaos all blended to make a cherished holiday story. Now and then, the elves consider bringing the recipe back, but they always recall that night of broken gingerbread limbs and sneaky mouse nibbles, and decide to keep it stored away… at least for the time being.

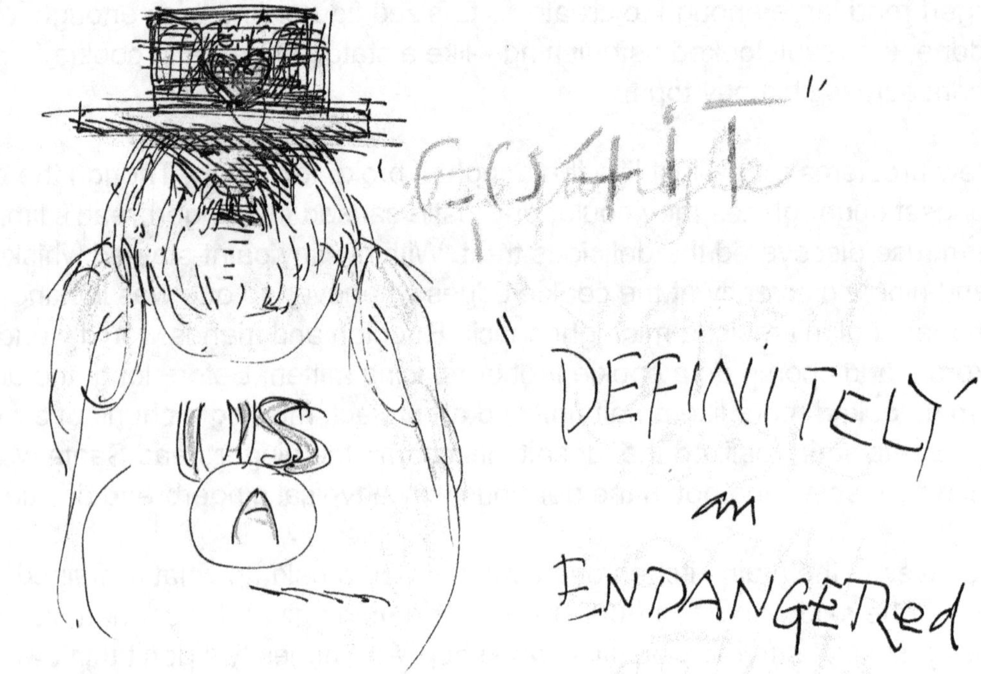

"DEFINITELY" an ENDANGERED SPECIES' some say

In the cozy twilight of a Northern summer, when the midnight sun drapes the Arctic horizon in soft pink and gold, Santa trades his heavy red coat for a simple tank top that reads "USA" and a pair of bright hibiscus-print shorts. On his head sits a woven straw hat, adorned with a small painted heart at the front—an easy, carefree style that could make anyone smile. At the North Pole, the elves affectionately call this "Santa's off-season look."

Yet there's something introspective in Santa's gaze tonight. Standing on a tuft of lingering snow, he studies the distant sky where winter clouds used to swirl. The gentle breezes from the melting ice sheets carry a faint memory of jingling bells, as if reminding him of the countless Christmas Eves he's embarked upon. But now, in this hushed summer moment, there are no sleigh rides, no reindeer pawing at the stables—just a wondrous stillness.

You see, many say that Santa is an "endangered species," a relic of childhood belief and fairy-tale wonder. They whisper that the modern, hectic world might overshadow those old stories, that grown-ups are forgetting to believe. Sometimes, these whispers drift up to the North Pole with the swirling wind, hinting that maybe Santa's time is fading.

But here, beneath the perpetual twilight of summer, Santa hears those rumors and only chuckles, a warm glow in his eyes. He knows that while grown-ups might doubt, the spirit of giving and hope still sparks in countless hearts. In every child's giggle at the jingle of a bell, or an elder's nostalgic sigh at the scent of pine, Santa feels that same timeless magic.

Standing there in his floral shorts, he thinks of all the stories—of laughter shared around a crackling fireplace, of families gathered under twinkling lights, of gifts given not just in boxes and ribbons, but in the form of gentle words and open arms. He recalls children's letters scribbled in bright crayons, each one brimming with honesty, wonder, and sometimes heartbreakingly simple requests ("Please let my friend be happy this Christmas," or "I wish my puppy would get better"). In every heartfelt wish, Santa finds a piece of the reason he exists at all: to nurture kindness in every corner of the world.

He steps forward, the crunch of snow and gravel beneath his sandals, and breathes the cool Arctic air. Even if times change and beliefs waver, Santa's heart is steadfast—like a candle that never truly goes out, even when it flickers. His "endangered" status, as some label it, only reminds him to cherish every moment of goodwill, to redouble his efforts in showing love, patience, and generosity wherever he can.

Many miles away, in cozier climates, someone might be reading or listening to the bedtime tales that paint his extraordinary life—tales where Santa lifts children's spirits, mends broken toys, polishes the sleigh, or even sails a boat to deliver presents to coastal towns. Those stories kindle a spark in each reader's heart, reviving memories of simpler times and gentle dreams.

And now, here at the end of this long series of bedtime adventures, Santa sets aside his own musings and turns his thoughts to you, the reader who's journeyed so far across these magical pages. If you're feeling a bit nostalgic or wistful, Santa hopes you'll remember this:

You are never too old to marvel at the first snowfall of winter.

You are never too grown-up to pause and feel gratitude for the love that surrounds you.

And you are never too busy to imagine reindeer hooves on the rooftop, or bright sleigh bells echoing in the night sky.

The season of giving, the hush of a cozy winter's night, the swirl of magic dust in a workshop—these things live on in each story told, each memory shared. They linger in every quiet moment when someone decides to be kind, just because it feels right.

Santa lifts his straw hat in a gentle salute. "Thank you," he murmurs to the fading sky, and to you, the dear soul who has read along, savoring every bedtime tale. In his eyes, you can glimpse your own cherished memories reflected back—images of friends and family, of lights on a tree, of warm cocoa and laughter on a chilly night.

A soft breeze ruffles the fringes of his flowered shorts, and he smiles. Maybe next Christmas will come sooner than we think, and maybe in the swirl of snow and starlight, you'll remember these stories—these glimpses of a timeless figure who, straw hat or red hat, always stands ready to remind us of the best in ourselves.

Before he turns to go, Santa quietly whispers a final wish into the twilight: that the sweet spirit of childhood, of wonder and belief, follows you through all the days to come. May your dreams stay vivid, your heart stay gentle, and your laughter ring like sleigh bells in the hush of an evening.

And with that, Santa pads away across the thinning drifts of snow, a contented figure in bright floral shorts and a heartfelt hat—proving that sometimes, magic lives most vividly in the off-season, waiting patiently in the wings until the world once again calls out for a little holiday cheer.

As you drift to sleep tonight, hold these stories close. Let them remind you that love, gratitude, and imagination are never truly endangered—they're the quiet sparks that light up the world, one soft moment at a time.

Goodnight, dear reader, and sweetest of dreams.

Bob Camblin in his Tír na nÓg studio

A NOTE ABOUT THE ARTIST

Bob Bilyeu Camblin (August 1, 1928 – December 4, 2010) was an American artist who emerged as a defining figure in the vibrant 1970s Houston art scene. Equal parts mystic, provocateur, and virtuoso, Camblin infused his watercolors, paintings, drawings, and prints with layers of hidden meaning, intricate detail, and a sly sense of humor that captivated audiences and puzzled critics alike.

www.ingramcontent.com/pod-product-compliance
Lightning Source LLC
Chambersburg PA
CBHW081356090726
47908CB00011B/2699

* 9 7 9 8 9 9 2 0 1 2 3 2 3 *